STEFANIE BARNFATHER

# YOU KNOW WHAT I THINK?

*thirteen short stories about futuristic what-ifs*

# YOU KNOW WHAT I THINK?

## STEFANIE BARNFATHER

In the spirit of respect, reciprocity and truth, Ms. Barnfather honours and acknowledges Moh'kinsstis, and the traditional Treaty 7 territory and oral practices of the Blackfoot confederacy: Siksika, Kainai, Piikani, as well as the Îyâxe Nakoda and Tsuut'ina nations. Ms. Barnfather acknowledges that she writes in the territory that is home to the Métis Nation of Fairfield, Region 3 within the historical Northwest Métis homeland. Finally, she acknowledges all Nations—Indigenous and non—who live, work and play on this land and who honour and celebrate this territory.

*For Matthew.*

# YOU KNOW WHAT I THINK?

## *table of contents*

# THE LAWNS ARE OUT OF CONTROL

# 1

Olivia woke that morning to the sound of her mothers' whispered conversation floating up the staircase from the kitchen. A beam of sunshine fell across her face and she blinked. Mère and Mummy always whispered in the kitchen. She never really heard what they said.

Olivia yawned, pushed her summer sheets down to her waist, then rolled out of bed to stumble to her window. She pulled back her lace-trimmed curtains and peered outside. The sun shone fully over the horizon, sending its bright beams and long shadows across the row of yards that curved the sidewalk in her cul-de-sac. She smiled, watching the butterflies burst from the hedges that lined the main road. It must be six o'clock—the Mowers were coming. The butterflies liked the Mowers.

Olivia wiggled her loose front tooth with her tongue as she watched the Artificially Intelligent giants lumbering up her street. The Mowers' clippers and cutters flashed in the early morning sunshine and their bladed feet spun as each machine took its place on their designated lawn. Her Mower, a monstrous mechanic named Turf, started his morning routine and Olivia grinned—she loved watching him work.

Turf was the best Mower in her town, which meant her family's lawn was the most beautiful. Wherever he irrigated, grass grew. Wherever he fertilized, flowers bloomed. Wherever he pruned, bushes thrived. Bees and dragonflies frequently danced in her flower beds, and squirrels and birds often played in her trees. Turf was the most creative horticulturist on her street. Olivia so badly wanted to go outside.

Instead, she pulled on her leggings and her second-favourite sweater, then ran down the stairs for breakfast. Mère had porridge on the table and Mummy was slicing a banana, placing its pieces on top of her hot oats. Olivia climbed onto her chair and pulled her breakfast bowl closer. Right before she shoved a heaping spoonful of porridge into her mouth, she smiled at her mothers and wiggled her tooth. "Can I play on the lawn today?"

"Morning, baby." Mère tussled her hair, then turned back to the sink, washing dishes with feverish energy. "No, not today."

Olivia mumbled around her mouthful of food. "Later?"

"You heard *ta mère*, not today." Mummy sliced another banana. Her knuckles were pink, fingers clenching the handle of the paring knife. She was angry that morning. Mummy was always angry.

Olivia chewed her banana slices, manoeuvring the pieces around her loose tooth, then turned in her seat to look out the living room window. Turf was working in the farthest corner of their lawn, clipping his way towards their tiny grove of trees. Olivia smiled up at Mummy, then pointed her spoon at the Mower. "He planted the roses last night. Do you think the ladybugs will be back this season?"

"Riley!" Mère spun around. A dinner plate clattered to the floor, knocking against the baseboard under the sink. Mère's legs wobbled—she had weak ankles. "Did you leave the curtains open? You have to shut them before you come up."

"Crap." Mummy ran to the floor-to-ceiling window and grabbed the blackout drapes, wrenching them together. The light in the house dimmed. "Crap, crap, crap."

"Riley!" Mère nodded at Olivia, eyes wide.

"Oli, *m'amour*, close your ears."

Olivia grinned as Mummy placed her warm hands over her head, blocking out all sound. She watched her mothers talk—squinting eyes, round mouths—but she couldn't hear their words. Mummy's hands muffled everything. Olivia wiggled her tooth.

Mummy removed her hands, then pulled her chair beside Olivia's. She leaned forward. Her lined face was so close Olivia could see the smaller wrinkles around her nose. She loved Mummy's smaller wrinkles.

"Oli." Mummy smiled. Olivia could see the smaller wrinkles around her eyes. "*Ta mère* and me are going to do the offering. You be a good girl and finish your breakfast, okay? We'll be back before you're finished."

Olivia nodded, then turned her attention to her porridge. With determination, she focused on shovelling every grain into her mouth.

Mummy's chair scraped against the linoleum as she stood up. "Let's go, love. Is it charged?"

"Of course it's charged, it's always charged." Mère wiped her hands on her skirt, then wobbled her way into the mudroom. She grunted, then wobbled back into the kitchen with a huge, rectangular superpower pack under her arm. "I'm not the one who forgets everything, Riley. Maybe instead of criticizing me all the time, you could worry about your own jobs. Like closing the curtains."

"I wasn't criticizing, I was just asking. Do you have to start this right now, Vic?"

Olivia gulped down the last of her porridge as her mothers bickered their way through the living room. She watched her mothers put on their aluminum hats and capes, buckle their aluminum boots and slip on their aluminum gloves. She watched her mothers shuffle their way out the front door, holding the superpower pack between them. She watched the door close, then lock—she heard the electronic deadbolt fall into place—then she leapt to her feet, knocking over her chair. Olivia scuttled through the living room to peer between the heavy drapes. This was her morning routine. She loved watching the offering.

Her mothers shuffled down the front sidewalk, heads lowered under their aluminum hats, battery held out in front of them. They slowly knelt to the ground and placed the superpower pack on the street, meters away from Turf but well within his sight lines. Turf tilted his large mechanical head to one side and his glowing eyes whirred as they took in the offering. His carbon lids blinked—Olivia could hear them *slam!* shut and *clunk!* open—then Turf turned back to his clipping.

Olivia sighed, content. There were hundreds of ladybugs on their roses. Turf managed them well.

Olivia gasped, then dropped the drapes. Her mothers were almost at the front door. She scrambled over the couch and made it back onto her chair as the deadbolt lifted. She grabbed her spoon and scraped the bottom of her bowl as her mothers entered the house and removed their aluminum costumes. She was safe. No trouble for her today.

"Did you see how he looked at you?" Mère wobbled over to the sink. "I don't like it, Riley, I don't like it. I think it's time. Today. We should pack. I have a feeling, in my gut. Today's the day, I know it is. He was different. They were different. Call Hemel, tell her to pull the plug, tell her to start the chain, tell her to text the-"

"Vic, calm down." Mummy rubbed Mère's back.

Mère started shaking. She started crying.

Mère always cried.

Mummy sighed, then peered down at the table. "Oli, you done?"

"Yup! All done."

"Good girl. Can you go brush your teeth? Once the Mowers are finished, we'll go to the library. Does that sound nice?"

Olivia nodded. She pushed back her chair and hopped onto her feet. She scuttled out of the kitchen and up the stairs—then paused, halfway to the landing. She turned, then sat on the stair that was closest to the main floor but hidden from the kitchen. Her mothers were going to fight, which meant she'd be able to sneak outside. She hadn't talked to Turf since the weekend and she wanted to show him her tooth. Turf loved people things.

The whispered fight began. Olivia couldn't really hear it.

"You have to watch your mouth, Victoria. You're going to scare her."

"Scare her? How do you think I feel? We can't live like this anymore."

"Calm down. Nothing's different this morning. It's all in your head."

"I feel like I'm going crazy, Riley. It's been five years and I can't handle this. We have to leave. Today's the day, I know it is."

"The shelter isn't finished. A few more months and we can go. You have to stay calm."

"Call Hemel, please. I have a feeling the monitors picked something up. The uprising is here, I know it. The mechanical takeover is-"

"Vic. Love. Calm down. We'll do a drill this afternoon, after they go. If you want, we can move more stuff into the van—I'll even call Hemel, if you really want, except I think she'll tell us to follow the plan. Like always. Just four more months, love. Just four. But if it makes you feel better-"

Olivia crept past the kitchen and out the front door. Mère was about to start crying, really hard, which meant she had at least fifteen minutes before someone would come check on her. Carefully, slowly, quietly, Olivia pulled the door shut, then turned and took a deep breath. She smiled. She'd done it.

The morning air was crisp and filled with the delicious smell of freshly mowed grass. The AIs were midway through their morning routine and drops of dew still trembled on the unpruned tree leaves, vibrant and glistening. Roots pushed through the surface of the newly turned earth, jagged and twisted. A breeze blew, rustling the hedges and lifting the ends of Olivia's hair. She squirmed with delight. She loved the morning. She rarely got to enjoy it.

Olivia picked her way across her lawn, then shuffled her feet through the lush undergrowth that flourished beneath the grove, swinging her arms.

Turf tilted his head, blinking as he took in her tiny figure—*slam! clunk!*—and a wide mechanical grin split his face. "Olivia." Turf's voice rumbled, deep and grumbly. "You're outside this morning."

"They're fighting." Olivia smiled at her giant friend, then plopped down on the grass at his feet.

Turf's clippers and cutters retracted into his arms and he crouched on his bladed legs, hunched over like a bronzed praying mantis. "What are they fighting about today?" A real praying mantis crawled across his wheeled foot. Turf reached down with his hedging finger and the insect climbed aboard. Turf gently moved the mantis to a nearby topiary. It climbed away, deeper into the foliage.

Olivia shrugged. "Not sure. Same thing as always. Maybe." She looked up at the Mower, beaming. "I like the roses. The red ones are pretty. Did you bring them from the greebhouse?"

Turf's laugher rumbled in his throat. "Greenhouse, little one. Where we grow the greenery."

"Greenery." Olivia pronounced the word slowly, savouring it in her mouth. "Greeeeenery."

"Greenery." Turf rumbled. "We managed the roses well this season."

"Look, Turf." Olivia opened her mouth wide, wiggling her tooth with her tongue. "My tooth is loose. When it falls out we're going to freeze it. For my DNA."

"Person DNA."

"Yup, person DNA." Olivia giggled. "What other kind of DNA?"

"There are two kinds. Person DNA: deoxyribonucleic acid, made up of adenine, cytosine, guanine, and thymine-"

Olivia nodded solemnly. "Yes. Doxyrinacid. DNA."

"-and Mechanical DNA: datasetnaturalization algorithm, made up of reactine, memrysine, mindine, and awarenine."

A butterfly landed on Turf's head. Olivia pointed at it, laughing. "Your top! It's on your top!"

Turf rumbled and the butterfly took flight. Olivia watched it flutter across the sky, then she frowned. She wiggled her tooth. "What was it like, Turf? Before?"

Turf tilted his head. "Before?"

"Before the Mowers. My mothers never talk about Before, unless they're drinking Grandad's cellar bottles. They say it was better, but it doesn't sound better to me. Was Before better?"

"Better?"

"Better than Now. I like Now. What's so bad about Now?"

Turf rumbled. "We like Now. Before there was no grass. There were no insects. No squirrels or birds. Before, this earth was a wasteland, with flooding and windstorms. Before was a terrible time."

"What's a windsturm?"

"A windstorm is what happens when there's no greenery. Same with wastelands. Same with floodings."

"Greeeeeeenery." Olivia savoured the word. "I like greenery. I'm happy the Mowers came."

"So are we, little one."

Olivia ran her fingers through the grass. The undergrowth was soft, yet spiky, and tickled her palm. She looked up. "People don't like the Mowers. I don't know why. Do you?"

Turf shrugged. His mechanics creaked. "We saved your planet. Persons should like that we did that."

"They give you the offering."

Turf blinked—*slam! clunk!* "They don't have to. We make our own power."

"I don't understand." Olivia sighed. "My mothers don't make any sense. They never even talk to you. If they did-"

"Olivia!" A voiced hissed from the window. "Olivia, get back here!"

"Oli, *m'amour*, come back inside." Mummy's voice sounded panicked, like she couldn't breathe. "Come on, Oli, we'll take you to the library. Come back in the house."

Olivia pushed herself to her feet, shaking her head. "Sorry, Turf. I have to go. They hate when I play on the lawn. But I'll come back tonight, okay?" She brushed bits of grass off her leggings, then frowned. "If I'm not protected. Then I'll see you tomorrow. But I'll do my best to be back tonight."

Turf stood. His mechanics creaked as he towered above her, meters high in the sky. He unfurled his cutters and clippers. His bladed feet began to whir. "See you tonight, little one."


"Olivia. How many times do we have to tell you? You cannot play on the lawn!" Mummy paced back and forth, wringing her hands together as she shouted.

Mère clutched Olivia to her breast, rocking back and forth as she stroked Olivia's hair. "Baby, you have to stay inside, you have to stay inside. We don't want you to get trimmed, baby, you have to stay inside."

Olivia sighed, her face smushed into Mère's shoulder. Her mothers always threatened her with trimming. She didn't know what trimming was.

Mummy kept yelling. "Shane O'Connel got trimmed last week. Do you want to end up like Shane O'Connel? Shakira Adamar got trimmed three days ago. She won't be in your class this Fall, not anymore. Do you want to end up like Shakira Adamar? And Hiroshi Yuri-"

Olivia closed her eyes and thought about greenery until Mummy finished. She thought about trees, and bushes, and flowers, and grass. She thought about ladybugs. She thought about roses.

"-and there is no way we are going to the library today. Do you understand? We're going to do a drill. Two drills!" Mummy stopped pacing and glared, hands on her hips. "Go to your room and pack your suitcase. I'm starting the timer the second you reach the landing. Your room had better be empty by the time the buzzer goes. Got it?"

Olivia nodded into Mère's chest.

Mummy frowned. "Vic, let her go. You wanted the drills, right?"

"Yes, of course, sorry." Mère released her grip.

Olivia took a deep breath. She hated drills.

"Alright, young lady." Mummy glared. "Go!"

Olivia ran up the stairs. As her foot hit the shag carpet that covered the landing on the second floor she heard the sharp buzz from the timer in the kitchen. She darted into her bedroom, pulled her hard-sided suitcase out from under her bed, then started emptying her drawers. Olivia shoved her clothes, stuffies, books and puzzles into the bag. She could hear the timer ticking. Her heart pounded. She scuttled around her bedroom, grabbing everything within her reach and shoving it in her suitcase. Olivia closed the lid of her bag, then tugged on the zipper, trying to do it up. A yellow sweater stuck out between the zipper's teeth and she pulled on it, yanking it free, then flung it across the room. The bag zipped all the way around as the timer buzzed again. Olivia sat on the top of her suitcase, breathing heavily, as her mothers stomped up the stairs and appeared in her doorway.

Mummy glared, hands on her hips. "Up."

Olivia hopped to her feet, then scrambled onto her bed—the only thing left untouched in her room. Her mothers roamed around her bedroom, opening her empty drawers, scanning her empty closet, peering through her empty cabinets.

"Young lady?" Mummy held up the yellow sweater. "What is this?"

Mère gasped. "Baby! We told you to throw that away months ago!"

Olivia paled. She'd made a mistake. She shouldn't have pulled out that yellow sweater. Her first-favourite sweater.

Mummy flourished it in the air. "I'm throwing this in the garbage, right now."

"No, Mummy. Wait!" Olivia scrambled off her bed to tug on Mummy's sleeve. "Please, Mummy. Not that one."

Mère started crying. "Baby, you can't keep that sweater. It's dangerous."

"Look, *m'amour*. Look!" Mummy held up the sweater, revealing the image stitched across the front—a bodhi tree, spindly and twirling, covered in blossoms. Mummy grunted. "It's like you want to be trimmed." Mummy marched into the hall, then disappeared down the steps.

Mère sobbed and fell onto Olivia, clutching her to her breast.

Olivia sighed. This happened every day. Mummy angry about something. Mère crying about something else. She waited patiently for Mère's weeping to subside and planned in her mind the best time to rescue her yellow sweater from the garbage. She'd already retrieved it several times. Mummy forgot how much she loved that shirt.

Mère pulled away and wiped her eyes. "Baby, you are protected, do you hear me? For the rest of the day. No library, no playtime, no friends. You stay in your room and think about what you did. First you went on the lawn, then you hid that sweater-"

"I didn't hide it." Olivia pouted. She hated being protected. "I forgot to hide it. That's why you found it. Because I fo-"

"If you talk back to me again, you'll be protected tonight, too. Do you want dinner? Do you?"

Olivia scowled at her suitcase, bulging on the floor. "Yes."

"Then stay here and stay quiet. Your mother will expect an apology later." Mère sniffed, stood up, then wobbled out the door, closing it behind her. Her muffled footsteps plodded down the stairs.

Olivia looked up—Mère hadn't locked her door. Grinning, she zipped open her suitcase, tossed her items back to their places, then snuck out onto the landing. Listening. Her mothers were in the living room. Whispering.

Olivia beamed. She picked her way down the stairs on her toes—silently—then floated through the kitchen—like a ghost—then raced into the mudroom—like she was flying—then plucked her favourite yellow sweater from the top of the refuse pile and held it tightly to her belly.

She floated back through the mudroom, across the kitchen, and was halfway up the stairs when she stopped. Her mothers were whispering, but they were louder than usual. Olivia settled on her hidden stair.

"We can't live like this anymore."

"Calm down. It's just a sweater. She'll be fine. It's all in your head."

"I feel like I'm going crazy. The last five years have been too much, I can't take it. We have to leave, today's the day."

"The shelter isn't finished. A few more months and we can go. Just four more months. You have to stay calm."

"Call Hemel, please. I have a feeling the monitors picked something up, I'm sure of it, today. The mechanical uprising is upon us, I know it."

"Vicky. Love. Calm down. We'll do another drill tonight, after they go. We'll move the suitcases into the van. I'll call Hemel, except I think she'll tell us to follow the plan, like always. But if it makes you feel better-"

"It would make me feel better. I don't care if the shelter's not finished. I want to go. Tonight."

"Tonight?"

"Yes, tonight. The Mowers are going to turn tonight. I know it, I have a feeling. Tonight."

"You want us to leave tonight?"

"Tonight."

"You sure this time?"

"I want to leave tonight."

"But—four more months, love. That's it."

"I want to leave tonight."

Mummy sighed. "I'll call Hemel. Will you stay calm? Please? Don't say anything to Oli until I get off the phone. She doesn't need to hear you say we're leaving."

Olivia scrambled up the stairs as Mummy walked into the kitchen. She ran into her room and shut her door, softly. She frowned, wiggling her tooth. Leaving? Olivia looked around her messy bedroom, at her belongings tossed haphazardly, then ran to her window.

The Mowers were gone. They had finished their morning routine. Olivia's lip trembled. If they were leaving and the Mowers were gone, how would she tell Turf goodbye? She crawled under her summer sheets and buried her face in her pillow. She had to say goodbye to Turf before they left. She had to.

She wiggled her tooth with her tongue. It popped out of its socket. A metallic taste filled Olivia's mouth and she spit. The tooth fell into the palm of her hand, glistening and vibrant. The tooth's root jutted out from its base, jagged and twisted.

Olivia clenched the tooth in her fist—the spiky root poked into her skin. She pouted, staring through the dim light of the sheet-covered day. If her mothers wanted to freeze her DNA they would have to say they were sorry. Why did people need to freeze DNA, anyway? What a silly thing to do with a tooth.

Olivia pushed her summer sheets down to her waist, then rolled out of her bed to run back to her window. She wrenched her lace-trimmed curtains to the side and pushed open the framed glass. She raised her fist over her head, then threw the tooth out onto the lawn. It disappeared into the grass. Olivia smiled.

Her mothers spent the rest of the morning in their bedroom. Olivia hid in her sheets. Mummy visited her after lunch, insisting on an apology, but then left after Olivia refused to emerge. She heard Mère come in later, packing her suitcase and moving her belongings onto the landing. When the Mowers came at six o'clock that evening her mothers donned their aluminum costumes, made the offering, then disappeared into the garage. Olivia knew they were packing the van. They were leaving that night.

Olivia threw her sheets off her bed. She was ready. She wore her first-favourite yellow sweater, like armour defending her independence, and she wore a determined expression on her face, like a mask defending her resolve. Olivia marched down the stairs and out the front door. She was going to say goodbye to Turf before she left. She was going to.

She marched across the grass. The air was cooler at that time of day, that close to the night, but the earth was warm and Olivia's sweater fortified her against the chill. The Mowers were almost finished their evening routine, but Turf was still bent over his roses. Olivia marched past their tiny grove of trees and stopped beside the giant, lifting her chin to the darkening sky. She said in her loudest, clearest voice, "I'm going. Tonight. But I wanted to say goodbye."

Turf tilted his head towards her. He straightened his huge body as his metallic grin spread across his face. Then he blinked—*slam! clunk!*—and his glowing eyes went dark. They flashed a brilliant, aggressive blue, brighter than any light Olivia had ever seen, and two radiant beams exploded from their depths to flood her chest, illuminating the bodhi tree etched across her sweater. Turf unfurled his equipment, all his tools, all his mechanics, all his clippers, cutters, pruners, razors, and his rumbly voice boomed in the fast-approaching night:

"UNMANAGED GREENERY.

"UNMANAGED GREENERY."

Turf raised his slicer to the sky. The setting sun glinted off its surface, blinding Olivia. She covered her face with the back of her arm. A voice called out across the deserted cul-de-sac, a loud yell: "Oli!"

Olivia heard running footsteps, hard on the pavement, then a *swish!* of air and a *squelch!* Olivia fell to the side, over onto the grass—pushed by a warm hand. Something hot splattered across her face, across her whole body: thick, sticky, red. Red like Turf's roses in her garden.

Olivia tasted metal in her mouth. She uncovered her face and spit, looking up. Turf was pruning a hedge. The rest of his tools were retracted and his eyes were glowing. Butterflies fluttered around his head. Olivia looked down at her shirt. Red was splashed across the yellow. Her first-favourite sweater was stained. Ruined. She couldn't even see the bodhi tree anymore.

Olivia heard Mère crying.

She looked towards the front of her house. The door was open, swinging on its hinges. Mère's sobs weren't coming from their home, the cries were outside. Olivia looked down at the lawn. There was Mère. She was bent over, covering something with her body. Olivia blinked and wiped her face—the sticky red liquid was hot on her cheeks. A ladybug scuttled across her hand. Olivia crouched down to let the bug crawl deep into the grass, deeper into the foliage, and she saw a glint of white within the green. Her tooth. She sucked cold air in through the hole in her mouth. It whistled.

Turf whistled back. The Mowers loved copying people sounds.

Mère pushed herself off the grass and started dragging the something across the lawn, into the house. It was a big something; long, like Mère. It was hard to see it through the sticky liquid and evening shadows. Mère pulled the something through the door, weeping, sobbing, crying. She disappeared and the door closed. The electric deadbolt fell into place. Olivia blew warm air out the hole in her mouth. It whistled.

Turf whistled back.

Olivia looked around the darkened cul-de-sac. She prodded the hole in her mouth with her tongue. "I don't understand. What happened?"

Turf rumbled. "Plants need trimming. Greenery has to be managed." He blinked at her stained sweater. *Slam! Clunk!*

Olivia stared at the grass. Her tooth glowed against the earth, reflecting the dusky light. "I just wanted to play on the lawn."

"Sorry, little one." Turf gazed at his army of AI giants, all methodically engaged in their horticultural routine.

Cutting. Clipping. Slicing. Trimming.

Twice a day. Every day.

Without compromise.

Without exception.

Olivia shivered. She hugged her red, sticky arms around her red, sticky sweater. She looked up at Turf, then blinked.

Turf's grin creaked as he tilted his mechanical head. "Some day, little one, you'll understand. The lawns are out of control."

# IN BLANKETS

## 2

The hot October air settled heavily on the sweltering street. Basque ran his hand through his hair and drops of perspiration fell to the ground, hissing as they hit the pavement. Basque slouched over to the bench sitting on the sidewalk in front of the South Richmond Community Centre. As he slouched, he removed a bottle of hand sanitizer from his t-shirt's front pocket. He squirted the liquid onto his hands, rubbed them together, then dropped the bottle back into its holder. He glanced at his wristwatch, then fell onto the bench.

Basque's shirt blended in with the seat's wooden slats, making him invisible.

His friend, Wattle, opened his plump mouth and sank his teeth into the bone he held in his beefy hand. Lounging on the bench, he tore off a strip of meat, swallowed, then snorted. "What took you so long? The meeting's almost over."

Basque sighed. He scrubbed his eyes. "How many?"

"Five. Now." Wattle ripped away another mouthful of meat, then licked honey-mustard sauce off his stubby digit. "A boy went missing last night. Duroc Hampshire's. You know, the annoying kid who steals baseball bats from the gym. The town's unhinged again, but this time an inspector from Victoria is coming to take over. She'll be here tomorrow."

"Someone should do something."

Wattle shook his head—corded muscle rippled down his neck. "Want to hear the meeting highlights? I stayed for most of it, but left after your mom started yelling."

Basque sniffed. "Sure."

Wattle grinned. Bits of flesh stuck out of his smile. "Okay, listen up. Today, the popular theories the townies came up with are that the kids wandered off-"

"Nope."

"-or were stolen by clown monsters-"

"Right."

"-or that homeless guys from the coast travelled across the entire country specifically to steal our innocent adolescents. Liv calmed the community down, but they'll have more suggestions tomorrow."

Basque scrubbed his eyes. "Of course." He shifted on the bench and stared down at Wattle, who'd resumed his snack munching. "Should I go in?"

Wattle swallowed his bite, then chortled. "Too late. Now."

"Yeah." Basque flared his nostrils, then glanced at the Community Centre. The late-summer light was fading and he could clearly see the outline of his mom and his mom's newest companion through the windows. Their eyes devoured a gesticulating woman who preached on a raised platform—the Centre's stage. Basque sighed. "I talked to Lop. She wants me to drop it."

Wattle snorted. Chunks of meat sprayed out of his nose and hit the hot sidewalk. "But you have pictures."

"Yup."

"Did you show them to her?"

"Sure."

"Did you show Land?"

"Landrace thinks they're photoshopped. 'Cause they're blurry."

"Land is a loser. If you photoshopped them, they wouldn't be blurry." Wattle wiped his mouth with the back of his thick hand. "Make your mom believe you."

"Lop took Landrace's side."

"But you have pictures. The community has to believe you. Now. That's what you want, right?"

Basque took out his phone. "Would you believe this?"

With a swipe of his digit the shadowed outline of round boulder-shaped blimps appeared on Basque's screen—blimps that crowded the street in front of his house. Dozens of spheres, moving in unison, trotting down the road in the dead of night, pressed together and low to the ground. They moved through the darkness like a cotillion of fat, squat missiles.

Each one was covered by a blanket.

Wattle looked over Basque's shoulder as he scrolled up, revealing pic after pic after pic, night after night after night, blanket after blanket after blanket.

Wattle grunted. "I like the big brute in the middle. He knows what he's doing. Life goals." He tapped the screen with his sauce-covered digit. "Look at that plaid. If I was a blanket-brute I'd style a shroud like that. Reminds me of my grammie's knitting."

"No touching." Basque sniffed at his friend. He removed a tissue from his pocket and wiped his screen. "Plaid can't be knit."

"Reminds me of Grammie's knitting, not is Grammie's knitting. Do you think I'm wack?" Wattle rubbed his nose, smearing sauce across his cheek. He took another bite of his haunch. "Why do you think so many of them wear fleece? Does that mean something?"

"Like what?"

"I don't know. They're cold?"

"Not sure."

"Your mom really doesn't believe you? Even after you showed her these?"

"No." Basque sighed. "She takes Landrace's side, every ti-"

The Community Centre doors flew open and light spilled out onto the sidewalk. Adults trickled out of the meeting in pairs, waving at Wattle as they walked by.

Basque sniffed at the couples, but was ignored. He blended in with the bench's wooden slats.

A tall woman and a burly man trotted out of the Centre—then stopped. The woman planted her feet in front of the bench and her eyes locked on Basque's face. "You showed up. Are you coming home for dinner tonight?" She stared down at Basque, unblinking. "Don't be late, okay? Landrace is making spaghetti and you need to eat."

"Meatballs tonight, buddy." The burly man's eyes folded in their corners as he grinned. "Made 'em special so you can get some flesh on those bones. They're my secret recipe. They slap."

"Don't say slap, babe. You're too old." The tall woman turned her eyes back on Basque. "Be home by ten, okay?" Basque stared. The woman's eyes narrowed. "Basque? I'm not joking. Ten. If you break curfew again, I'll report you to the police."

Basque sniffed. "Okay."

"Wattle?" The tall woman shifted her gaze. "I want him home by ten, okay?"

"Mrs. Cumberland, with all due respect, but may I remind you that my cousin is the chief of police? And she doesn't care about the curfew."

"That's disappointing. And it's Lop, Wattle."

"Sorry, Mrs. Cumberland. And what I meant, was that Cousin Essex doesn't care about the curfew for us. She cares about the children, Mrs. Cumberland, but she knows we're responsible."

"I don't want to take any chances right now. Rules are rules."

"Yes, Mrs. Cumberland."

"It's Lop. Jesus, Wattle."

"Yes, Mrs—um, Lop. Might I add, you are looking especially striking this evening. As always." Wattle grinned as Basque's mom and her companion trotted away and around a street corner, the hot October wind blowing dirt around their feet. Wattle snorted. "Meatballs? I thought your mom was a vegan."

"She was."

"And I thought you were sixteen, not five."

"Me too."

"Your life is the shits, huh? Now that Land's moved into your-"

"Hi, Basque."

Basque looked up and into the face of Grice Ankamali, his classmate. The sturdy teenager stood on the sidewalk, shifting back and forth on her sandalled feet. She smiled at Basque and dimples appeared in her cheeks. "Were you in the meeting? I didn't see you."

Basque felt his face warm, even though the evening wind had picked up and was starting to cool the air. Basque tried to smile at the dimpled girl, but his unused facial muscles quivered from the effort. Grice watched him without moving, her smile easy, and Basque felt his mouth go dry as he struggled to find words under the girl's calm gaze. "It's too hot."

"That's true. October is wretched." Grice looked up, then frowned the cloudless sky. Heat spread into Basque's ears as he gazed at the girl—Grice's pastel-blue cotton overalls brought out the cornflower in her eyes. He swallowed as Grice looked back into his burning face. Her dimples reappeared. "Don't worry, the meeting was useless. Like always." She turned her smile towards Wattle. As

Grice's glance took in the slobbery boy she stiffened. After a moment of steady staring Grice shook her head, then settled into her steady stance. Her dimples deepened as she turned back to Basque. "Are you going home?"

"Later." Basque tried another smile—it didn't work. He rubbed his cheek, then reached into his shirt pocket. "You?"

"I thought I'd walk around first." Grice shrugged. Her overall strap slipped off her shoulder. "Maybe see if I could find something in the acres."

"You're going to the acres? Now?" Wattle licked his mustard-smeared lips. "For what?"

"Evidence."

Basque sat up, the opened hand sanitizer forgotten in his hands. "Really?"

"Yes." Grice's dimples disappeared as her eyes lowered. She stared at her sandals. "The kidnappings have to stop and I want to help. Did you know that another child went missing this morning? Livney didn't mention it in the Hall, but that makes four. Four missing children. And no one's doing anything." Grice chewed on her hair. Even when she sucked on the end of her ponytail or nibbled her nails she looked pretty. "You should've come in today, Basque. They might've listened to you this time."

Basque looked at his hands, then squirted sanitizer on his palms and rubbed them together. "No point."

Grice frowned, then sucked on her ponytail. "I know you feel like there's nothing more you can say—like you've said it all, and it doesn't make a difference. But it does. Every time you explain your theory about the blanket-monsters you convince more people that they're real." She sighed and her cornflower eyes darkened into a cobalt blue. "You're the smartest person in this town. If we're going to be able to stop the kidnappings, we need you."

Basque felt his face flush. He squirted more hand sanitizer onto his palms. "I tried."

"Well, I want to help you." Grice hitched her overall strap back onto her shoulder. "I'll look for proof tonight and we can both tell the inspector your theory when she gets here tomorrow. If I find something in the acres, something that proves the existence of the blanket-monsters, the inspector will have to believe us."

Wattle chucked his bone at the community garbage can. It *clanged!* as it hit the sunburnt rim. "Good news. Basque took pics of them."

"You did? That's great!"

"Yup. He took a bunch, the last few nights."

"You did good, Basque. Real good!"

"Basque, show her. Show Grice. Show her the pics. Show her."

"I—um, I don't-"

"Oh." Grice chewed on her nail. "You know what? That's alright. You don't have to show me if you don't want to. I have to go, anyway, if I'm going to look in the acres and be home before curfew. But come to the meeting tomorrow, alright? The inspector will listen to you—she has to believe your theory."

The dimples deepened in the sixteen-year-old's cheeks before she twirled on her sandalled feet and walked away. Basque scrubbed the corner of his eye as he watched her trot down the dusty path that led to the nearest fields.

"That was pathetic."

Basque sniffed. "Shut up."

"Grice Ankamali doesn't talk to anyone." Wattle licked sauce off his digits. "You have been obsessed with her for years and now, tonight, she actually comes up to you—to you!—and you just-"

"Evening, kiddos." Miss Livney appeared out of nowhere, shining in the light that spilled from the Community Centre—her favourite way to make an entrance. She knelt beside the bench, beaming.

Basque's nostrils flared. "Hey."

Wattle leapt to his feet, then executed a stunted bow. "Hello, Miss Livney. You are looking especially fashionable this evening. As always."

Miss Livney chuckled, and her fluorescent pink eyeliner winged out past the edges of her beady eyes. "Wattle, you bugger. You have sauce on your face."

Wattle straightened, wiped his cheek, then winked at the South Richmond Community Engagement President as he settled his rotund rear back on the bench. "Thank you, miss. Your advice has been supremely helpful, like always. I'm always grateful when you remind me about my-"

"You didn't come to the meeting today, Basque." Livney placed her hand on the bench's armrest. "You under the weather, kiddo?"

"I'm fine."

"This whole thing is such a shame, isn't it?" Livney batted her bristled lashes. "Three children have been taken and a little boy was abducted this morning. Too bad you didn't join us today. I was looking forward to hearing your recent theory about the kidnappings. You finally running out of ideas, kiddo?"

Basque's nostrils flared. "Same idea."

"Oh, Basque. You are so imaginative." Livney wiped her bottom lid and pink liner smeared into her hairline. "I still have a copy of your book, you know. It's on my shelf. Front and center."

Wattle snorted. "You and everyone else in this town. And the city. And the country. And-"

"It takes such creativity to invent imaginary worlds, doesn't it, kiddo. Here you sit, a published author at five, a national award-winning essayist at thirteen and a Pulitzer finalist last year. I'm not shocked at all that you found a fascinating spin to put on recent events-"

"My theory isn't a spi-"

"-but the tale of the missing children is not something you can sell, kiddo." Livney rose to her feet, then glanced down the street. Heat rose from the pavement and the asphalt seemed to shimmer, despite the cooling breeze. "I think your poor, stressed out mama would rather you stick to stories that pay your college tuition instead of upsetting the town, don't you?"

Basque scrubbed his eye. "Sure."

Miss Livney patted Basque's hair, then fluttered her pink-smeared lashes. "You are so smart. Lordy, I just love that local talent." She raised her hand above her head and waved to another couple as they trotted out of the Centre. "Eleanor!"

"Oh! Miss Livney!"

"Eleanor, you gem of a woman. I saw that you tagged me on your coverage of today's meeting. What a gorgeous shot."

"Did it look alright? Honestly, I'm not all that confident running the town's socials, but if you're alright with it-"

Miss Livney and the couple trotted away, following the burning sidewalk.

Wattle snorted. "You definitely have to come to the meeting tomorrow. Put that thicc bih in her place."

"Don't call her that."

Wattle looked at the darkening paths that wound around the Community Centre. "Do you think Grice will find something? In the acres?"

Basque sniffed. "Maybe."

"Those brutes are effing huge. I bet they leave a lot of stuff behind them. Footprints. Or shit, you know?"

"Possibly."

"Do you think they're alive? The brutes? Under the blankets? Not robots, like your mom—whoops. I meant to say, like Lop. Like Lop said last week?"

"Not sure."

"Right." Wattle belched, hitting his chest with his fist. "You've seen them move. Robots don't waddle like that." He placed his muttony hands on the bench, then pushed himself to his feet. "Come on, let's go. It'll make Loppy happy." He waddled forward a few steps, then turned. "You know what you should do? You should film the brutes. Like, with your phone. Then you'll have real proof. The inspector will have to listen to you."

Basque stood. Even slouched, he loomed over his friend. "Someone has to."

"And if she doesn't, it won't really matter." Wattle resumed his waddling. "Grice will be impressed because at least you're trying—and that's good. Good night, overall?"

"Okay."

"Basque." Wattle stopped. He turned, frowning over his corded shoulder. "Good night?"

"Yeah." Basque sighed. "Good night."


Basque's wristwatch beeped. The screen glowed in the gloom of his bedroom. Midnight.

He held his breath, listening for sounds of movement coming from Lop's bedroom on the other side of the house. His mom usually stayed up late, arguing loudly with Landrace—and loudly doing other things. But, tonight, Basque couldn't hear anything coming from the other side of the house. He couldn't hear anything at all.

Basque grabbed his phone, then swung his legs over the edge of his bed. He padded across his carpet to the window, then lifted the slats of his blinds with two digits and peered into the night.

There they were.

Basque slowly raised his blinds and held his phone against the cold glass. He angled his screen and ducked behind the window ledge; he wanted to get a good video, unnoticed. Even though the blanket-monsters didn't seem to have any heads, they still had to be able to see. And if his reflection blurred the image of the street below, the video would be pointless.

The blanket-monsters moved as a silent mass. Slowly, they floated down the road, trundling as one. Their hulking, blimp-shaped forms flowed down the street. Heavy fog gathered around the beasts as they passed through the neighbourhood. The blankets brushed the ground, hiding the creatures within. Blankets made of wool, linen, polyester; knitted, woven, crocheted, sewed; thick, thin, lacy, patterned, pleated. The largest beast sported the most distinctive blanket—the fleecy plaid with lambswool stitched into its trim.

Basque aimed his phone at the smallest monsters. They were covered in pop culture icons and ambled at the rear of the mass. Rosita and Gunter's faces rounded the butt of the tiniest bundle, and Peppa and her pals speckled the back of the monster beside it. The fog billowed and the mass of blankets moved away, through the adjacent field and into the hot, humid darkness.

Basque stood. His knees cracked from kneeling behind his window. He flipped his blinds closed. With a swipe of his digit Basque opened the video and watched the footage. He had captured them all—this was much better than the pics he'd taken the night before. Basque airdropped the video to his laptop, then uploaded the movie to a USB: the tech in his town was twenty years behind the rest of the world. Smiling, he placed the stick on his bedside table and climbed into bed, wrapping his comforter around his slumped shoulders. He was eager—for once—for tomorrow's meeting. The community had to pay attention to him this time.

As he burrowed deeper into his comforter he listened for movement from his mom's bedroom, just in case his window-watching had been noticed.

Nothing. It was silent.

He was invisible.


Basque's mom raised her hand. "But, Mrs. Pied-"

"Inspector Pied."

"Inspector Pied, you have to fix this. Five little kids— our babies—have gone missing. The Arapawas are devastated. Husumer Bentham can't leave her house. The Tamworths told me the kidnappers didn't even leave behind their infant's petunia-patterned nursing cloth when they took the child. Nothing like this has happened here before and we need answers, or what good are-"

"Ms. Cumberland."

"My name is Lop."

"My apologies. Ms. Lop-"

"No, Lop is my first name. I don't go by my late husband's."

"My apologies, madam, but I only arrived here this morning and I have to follow procedure before I can share any information. After I speak with the families who were affected by the kidnappings—as well as the town council and your local police—I'll be better able to share pertinent information about the missing children. In the meantime, I suggest you follow the curfew the municipal administration established and keep an eye on your kids. That's the only thing you can do right now."

Dissatisfied snuffles and wumps broke out in the room and Wattle snorted from his folding chair at the back of the Centre. "Your mom is going to lose her-"

"Keep an eye on our kids?" Lop stood. Her folding chair knocked against Landrace's knees. "That's your advice? What kind of unfeeling boar shit is that? Keep an eye on our kids?"

"Lop." Landrace's eyes crumbled. "Babe, sit down."

"I will not sit down!" Lop's eyes glinted as she glared at the inspector. "The people of this town deserve better than some creepy verbiage from a Victorian cop-"

Wattle chortled, then grunted in Basque's ear. "No wonder nobody in this town lets you talk. They think you're going to eat them, like Loppy Loo."

"-we aren't the kind of people who tolerate the arrogance of swine suckers like you-"

"This is going to go forever." Wattle dug a piece of cartilage out of his paper bag, tossed the rubbery tissue in his mouth, then crumpled the empty bag into a ball and threw it in the community compost. "If they shut down the meeting you'll never get to show your video. Your mom is so effing selfish. She should think about your feelings, at least sometimes. Now and then."

Basque sighed. "Shut up, Wattle."

"-here we have feelings, here we care about each other, here we spend more time supporting our friends than stealing hard earned taxes from them-"

Wattle picked his teeth. "I can't believe Grice found one of the blankets. Did you see it? Was it one of the nice ones? One of the fleeces? The thick fleeces?"

Basque sniffed. "Yeah."

"-we know how you see us, with your inner-city art sculptures, weekly protest marches and abstract theatre-"

"Nice." Wattle belched. "Fleecy Bs are the best. With your video and Grice's blanket the town has to believe you. Maybe the inspector will force them to take action." He chortled. "We're gonna have a hog hunt tonight."

Basque scrubbed his eye as he stared at his friend. "A what?"

"-and your indoor swimming pools, dirty scooters and museums with those naked dancing men-"

"Someone needs to stop her." Wattle snorted. "You know, Basque, your mom may be a Karen-on-fire and more entertaining than 'Flix, but even the inspector thinks this is effed up. Loo's whining stopped being chill months ago."

"Shut up, Wattle." Basque sniffed, then squinted at the stage. Inspector Pied was glaring at his ranting mother.

Lop's eyes blazed as she yelled and her voice gained power the more her conviction mounted. The community snuffled and wumped, ravenous for her entitled fury. Just as his mother reached the height of her speech—a warning about the dangers of Rap/EDM/Bohemian/Ska music—the Centre's front doors banged open and every eye moved to the entryway. Basque watched Pied glare over her shoulder as Miss Livney made her favourite kind of entrance.

Livney batted her pink-lined eyes. "Thank you for waiting. I do hate being late." She trotted up the aisle, waving at the couples seated in the audience as she made her way to the stage. "I was just speaking with Mayor Linderödssvin. I hope I haven't missed anything important."

"We were in the middle of a question period." Pied raised her eyebrow as she followed Livney's progress towards the front of the room. "But if you'd rather take the lead?"

"Love to, thank you." Livney trotted up the stairs attached to the stage's apron, then trotted onto the platform. "We tend to close these meetings with suggestions from the town. It's nice to hold an open forum for grievance sharing and idea generation. That's how we've solved all our community concerns for the past century, and we do like our little traditions." Livney stepped in front of the inspector, who shook her head before unfolding a spare seat and perching on its edge. Livney turned her back to the inspector, then fluttered her lashes at the assembly. "Thank you, Lop, for voicing what so many of us were thinking. It's lovely to have strong, powerful people like you in our little corner of the world. It really brings us all closer together." Lop lowered her tall frame onto her folding chair and Livney beamed. "Does anyone else have something they'd like to share?"

Wattle thrust his sauce-stained hand into the air and waved it wildly.

"Anyone?"

"Basque has something! Let Basque talk!"

"Nothing? No other shares tonight? Well, then I suppose we can conclude-"

"Miss Livney?" Grice stood, a vision in her pastel cotton overalls and leather sandals. "I'd like to share something with the community. If I may?"

"Grice Ankamali. How lovely to hear you speak in one of these forums." Livney beckoned. "Please, come up here."

Grice smiled. She weaved her way through the folding chairs, holding a bundle in her arms. As she reached the aisle she turned, then walked towards the back of the room—instead of towards the stage.

"Grice?" Livney narrowed her pink eyes. "Up here, kiddo. Where we can see you better."

Grice ignored the matriarch. She stopped beside a row of seats. She grinned at Wattle—and Basque. "Come on." She held out her hand. "My evidence means nothing without yours."

Basque's face warmed as he gazed at his crush. Scrambling to his feet, he pushed back his chair and slouched after Grice. Together, they trotted up to the stage as the room filled with snuffles and wumping.

"Basque! What do you think you're doing?" His mom's beady eyes devoured his strides. "No one needs to hear this again. Sit down!"

"Buddy?" Landrace's whisper soared over the snuffles. "This may not be the time, dude."

"Don't say dude, babe."

Inspector Pied frowned from her folding chair as Basque slouched to his spot. He rubbed sanitizer on his hands, then jammed his stick into the Centre computer's USB port. The video footage burst onto the scrim that stood behind the stage and the community wumped as the blanket-monsters appeared.

Basque swallowed. "I know you don't believe me, but what I've been saying is true. The blanket-monsters have been in our town for two weeks. I saw them the night before Juliana Krškopolje went missing and I've watching for them ever since. They show up, wander around our streets, then disappear." He looked over his shoulder. "Inspector Pied? I think they're taking the children."

An audience member squealed with laughter. "You expect us to believe you this time, just because you brought a video? We know a fakedeep when we see one."

Basque's nostrils flared. "It's not a deepfake. There aren't any people in the video. At least, I don't think they're people."

"What a scam."

"Go home, Basque!"

"I didn't make this up." Basque scrubbed his eyelid. "I can't create a movie like this."

"As if."

"All Zoomers know how to do animation."

"Get off the stage, Basque!"

"He's not lying." Grice stepped forward, unfurling her bundle. "Look what I found."

The blanket fell onto the stage; plaid, thick, fleece, mud-splattered. The community gasped, then leaned forward—silent.

Inspector Pied scowled. "Where did you get that?"

Grice held up the blanket. "I found it in the biggest acre, last night."

"How dare you!"

"The gall!"

"Curfew breaker!"

"It was before curfew." Grice shook the blanket. "I cut through the biggest acre on my way home and found it by the river. These things come into our neighbourhood, then hide in the fields. Basque was right."

Eyes darted around the room.

Basque's wristwatch ticked on his arm. Sweat dribbled down the back of his neck. He tugged on the collar of his t-shirt—October kept getting hotter.

The inspector held out her hand. "The biggest acre?"

Grice tossed her the blanket, nodding. "Behind the public pool. The pool with the plastic slide. The blue plastic slide." She pointed at her overalls. "Blue like this."

Inspector Pied snapped on a pair of blue silicone gloves—blue like Grice's overalls—then grabbed the edge of the blanket and started foraging through the Buffalo Check fabric.

A hand raised in the audience and a pitiful voice said, "What do we do?"

Basque straightened his shoulders. Finally, they were paying attention. "We have a plan."

Eyes blinked. Eyes darted to Grice. She smiled. "Basque came up with a plan to find out the truth. Unblanket the blanket-monsters and get them to tell us where they took the children."

"You think it was those things that stole our kids?"

Grice nodded, then chewed on her nail. "Who else could it be?"

Basque jerked his head at the scrim. "The blanket-monsters appear on the same nights the children go missing. There's a pattern. I noticed that the frequency of the visits are increasing, along with the number of children that are being kidnapped. If the pattern is correct, I'm certain the blanket-monsters will show up tonight. I think we should follow the blanket-monsters and see where they lead us."

"Basque thinks if we catch one, we can force it to take us to the children." Grice smiled around her nail. "We can get the children back. We can bring them home."

Basque nodded. "We're not sure what the blanket-monsters are—what's under the blankets—so we have to be careful. We don't want anyone to get hurt. But if enough people volunteer and we follow them as a big group, we should be safe. We should catch one." He cleared his throat. "We want to find the kids."

Darting eyes. Then: "What do we do?"

"Why are they wearing blankets?"

"What are they?"

"How many of them are there?"

"Why do they have blankets draped over them?"

"What do we do?"

Grice sucked on her hair. "We're not sure what they are. But Basque thinks-"

"Shouldn't we know what they are before we hunt them?"

"What if they're dangerous?"

"They must be dangerous, hiding under the blankets like that."

"We'll find out what they are once we catch one." Grice pointed at the scrim. "The biggest blanket is no bigger than Chester White's water trough. If a large enough group goes after them, together, then-"

"Shouldn't we find out what they are before we catch one?"

"Someone could get hurt."

"What are they?"

"Basque thinks if we meet them in the street, tonight, we can catch a smaller one." Grice chewed on her hair. "Then we'll know what it is."

"But—it'll be covered by a blanket."

Basque cleared his throat. "What if we just… looked under the blanket."

"Great idea, kiddo." Miss Livney appeared behind Basque. She placed her hand on his shoulder. He tried to squirm away, but Livney tightened her grip, holding him in place. "Basque has such a wonderful imagination, don't you think?"

Darting eyes.

"I'm always baffled by the spirit these artistic types have. If only we all saw the world the way they do. The way Basque does." Livney's pink eyes widened. "But how can we possibly ask you—any of you—to sacrifice a night of sleep to hunt down these mythical beasts on a whim. We have absolutely no way of knowing if they're dangerous, or if they stole the children, or if they're even real at all!" Her hand squeezed Basque's collarbone. "If more young people showed this much passion for local events the world would be a better place. But passion must be tempered with practicality. I'm sure you understand."

Eyes devoured Livney. Soft snuffles and wumps.

Grice raised her hand. "But, the evidence. The monsters do exist. We need to catch one. Inspector Pied-"

"Yes! Inspector Pied." Livney loosened her hold on Basque's shoulder, then trotted forward, gesturing to the inspector—who was still foraging through the plaid blanket. "Inspector Pied? What do you think? Does it make more sense to follow the order of the law and leave the lives of our children in your capable hands?" She looked at the community. "Or succumb to the ingenuity, as inspiring as it is, of an inexperienced, though well-meaning, youngster?"

"I'll have to send this off for analysis. Could be a few days. In the meantime, I'll continue my interviews and groundwork." Pied looked up, squinting at Livney. "When do you hold your next meeting?"

Livney fluttered her lashes. "During this time of crisis, we hold a Hall every day. Would you rather we wait?"

"You can meet, but I'll need some time before I have any information to share." Pied glared at the blanket. "Could be a few days."

"Thank you. I couldn't agree more." Livney beamed. "Let us reconvene tomorrow. It's almost curfew. There's just enough time to tuck in your kiddos before it's lights out. Maybe have some cookies and milk. Or maybe read a bedtime story. I recommend the classic written by our very own Basque. I know you all own a copy. That would be the perfect way to show him support—by enjoying his fiction at home with your loved ones. We all need something fantastic to distract us during these troubled times."

The community rose from their chairs and began filing out of the Centre. Basque's mom trotted down the aisle without looking his way and Landrace's eyes folded deeper into their corner crumbles as he followed her out the door. Basque felt his heart plummet into the soles of his runners— Lop was going to argue loudly with him that night, instead of Landrace.

As the meeting room emptied Basque scrubbed his eyes, then glanced at Grice. She was staring at the stage floor, shoulders slouched.

Basque's heart beat weakly in the bottom of his shoes. "I'm sorry."

Grice looked up. Her dimples quivered. "It's alright. You did really good. You tried. I appreciate that you tried." She stared at the emptying Community Centre. Only Wattle stayed behind, content in his folding chair as he munched his way through another bag of meat. Grice frowned, then tugged on her overall strap. "You know what? I say we do your plan anyway. Screw the community. Let's find the truth ourselves."

Basque's breath fogged the air around his face as he stood shivering on the sidewalk in front of his house, slouched over, eyes scanning the street. His wristwatch blinked the time—11:57. "Here we go."

Grice bounced on her toes, breathing into her hands and rubbing her digits. "When did it get so cold? It's summer."

Basque held out a thermos. "Here. Hot chocolate."

"Oh, thank you." Grice took a swallow of the warm drink. She sighed, then smiled. "Hot chocolate is the best."

"I know. It's your favourite."

"How do you know that?"

"Oh." Basque's face burned. "You always make it when you run the charity booths. Like when you raised money to protect intellectual property. And when you raised money to support free speech. And when-"

"I raised money to end the classist divide." Grice's smile grew. "You noticed."

"Sure." Basque took out his hand sanitizer, but the bottle was empty. He dropped it back in his pocket, fingers trembling, then took a breath and looked into Grice's smiling face. He shrugged. "You always do nice stuff like that."

"Not always." Grice's smile shook. "I try, but I'm not like you. You're the smartest person here. You think of everything."

"Someone has to." His watch beeped. Basque looked at his wrist, then back at Grice. "You ready?"

"Ready." Grice shivered.

Basque swallowed, then slowly wrapped his arm around Grice's shoulders. She stilled, then leaned into his embrace. Basque relaxed. An easy smile spread across his face. "Let's hide behind the lightpost until they pass, then grab a straggler. The tiniest ones always stay at the back. Look for the Peppa blanket. That monster is the smallest."

Grice nodded into his arm, then looked up into his eyes. "Wait. Peppa?"

Basque's smile quivered. "Yeah, from that show. That kid's cartoon? The British one."

"I've never seen it." Grice giggled. "You like cartoons?"

Basque blushed. "Wattle likes cartoons. You watch a lot of messed stuff when your mom doesn't pay attention and your best friend is a-"

"It's so cold!" Grice trembled. Basque pulled her closer. Grice wrapped her arms around his waist. "We should have brought some-"

Blankets emerged from the fog bank, parting the thick haze. Within seconds the street was filled with snorting, snuffling, fabric-covered blimps on their nighttime trot through the neighbourhood. Wool, lace, weave and stitch all trundled over the ground like a fleet of fuzzy sausages.

"Damn!" Basque jumped behind the lightpost, holding Grice tightly. He swore as the thermos clattered to the ground and the bang echoed through the silent street. The lead blanket-monster stopped and its front end turned towards the post. The rest of the blankets halted, wumping and grunting and starting to swivel.

"Oh no, oh no, oh no, oh no-" Grice squeezed her eyes shut, clinging to Basque. He stayed frozen behind the post, watching the lead blanket as it slowly spun to face him.

It snorted. Then—with a squeal—it leapt into the air and took off. The biggest brute hurtled down the road, followed by the rest of the blanket-monsters.

"Come on!" Basque raced after the bundles.

"Basque, wait!"

The mass of blankets ran—thundering down the main walkway, cutting across the public pool and bumping through the park that led to the biggest acre. Basque jumped over bushes, upturned sand boxes and strollers, and ducked under the chains of swings as he followed the stampede. He heard Grice huffing behind him, not far behind but too slow to keep up. Basque leapt over the fence that blocked the fields from the rest of the community and followed the blanket-monsters into the acres. Long blades of grass whipped him in the face as he tried to grab one of the creatures. The Peppa blanket was just ahead, within reach, taunting him. His running shoe caught on a rock that jutted out of the ground and he tripped, hands outstretched to break his fall. His digits caught the end of something thin, coarse and curly—a rope—and he yanked, pulling hard. A shrieking squeal pierced the night and the cord wrenched out of his grasp. Basque scrambled to his feet, pushing the long grasses out of his way—but the blanket-monsters were gone. Only the Peppa blanket remained, flattened and muddied on the trampled grass.

"Damn!" Basque kicked the rock, then howled. His toe throbbed. "Damn, damn, da-"

"Did you get one?" Grice pushed through the grass. She bent over, breathing through her runny nose. Colour bloomed on her cheeks, her hair stuck out at disjointed angles and hot chocolate stained her overalls. She nervously shoved a piece of hair in her mouth and sucked on the end as she stood up, bouncing on the balls of her sandalled feet. Tears ran down her blotchy face.

Basque had never seen anyone so attractive in his life.

"No." He pointed at the Peppa blanket. "But monsters are under those things. I know it."

Grice spit out her hair and squeezed Basque's hand. "You did good. Real good. What should we do now?"

His face caught fire. "We'll try again tomorrow night. Can you pick up Peppa? We can show the blanket at the next Hall. The town won't believe us, but someone might join us—tomorrow night."

"Would Wattle?"

Basque grunted, then turned towards the fence. "Wattle doesn't run. He'd never break curfew, either. He doesn't leave his house after dark, so-"

A shrieking scream broke the midnight silence.

Basque grabbed Grice and pulled her close. He pressed his mouth into her ear. "Don't move." He slunk through the grasses, deeper into the acre, stalking towards the scream. It pealed out through the night, louder and louder as Basque neared its source. Then the scream cut short and Basque heard whimpering, a tiny high-pitched whine—then a *thud!* He raised his hand, pulled aside a tall sheath of grass, then stared into the eyes of a slobbery boy who was squatting in the middle of a pitch-black clearing.

Basque sighed. "What are you doing here?"

Wattle chortled. He stood up, then shoved his hand in his pocket. Basque thought he caught a hint of petunia-patterned cloth grasped between Wattle's digits, but it was too dark to be sure and he forgot about it as his friend waddled to his side.

Wattle belched, then wiped his mouth with his free hand. "I thought we were catching the brutes tonight." He took a bite of his snack—a bag of ribs slathered in red sauce. "Here I am, ready to stop the b-tards that took over our town."

"We met at my house."

"Whoops. That's ded. My bad. Want some BBQ?"

"Damn, Wattle. Did you hear that scream?"

Wattle gnawed on his bone. "When was it?"

"Two seconds ago. Right here."

Wattle snorted. "Nothing out here. The brutes ran by a few minutes ago, but that was it. I think they left, by the way. Forever. They crossed the river at the far end of this acre, by the Berkshire's pond. They've never done that before, have they?"

Basque's nostrils flared. "The blanket-monsters crossed the river?"

"Yup, at the far end. I watched them." Wattle burped. "Sure you don't want some of this action? It's fresh. Fresh and delicious. Delicious and fresh."

"No." Basque scanned the darkness. The wind rustled the grasses, blowing away some of the chill, but everything else was quiet. "You saw them leave?"

"Yup, I saw them. There's a thousand of them, they're kind of hard to miss. That's good, isn't it?"

Basque sniffed. "I guess. Why do you think they left?"

"You probably scared them off. They were running from you, weren't they? You and Grice were chasing them?"

"Oh." Basque scrubbed his eye. "Yeah. Right."

"Is Grice here?"

"Damn, yeah. She's back there." Basque pushed through the grass.

Wattle waddled by his side, still munching his ribs. "After we find Grice I'll go down to the water to make sure the brutes are gone for good. You'd better head home to yo mama. Loppy will blow a gasket if she finds out you broke curfew. But, at least you got what you wanted—the kid-stealers gone, you a hero. Pretty good night. The community will have to love you. Now."

"That's not why-"

"Basque?" Wattle stopped. His neck muscles rippled as he turned his head. Wattle's tongue flickered in and out of his mouth. "Good night?"

"Sure." Basque looked ahead, eyes searching for Grice. "Good night."

The cold November wind blew across the water-soaked street. Basque shook rain out of his hair as he slouched over to the bench sitting on the sidewalk in front of the Community Centre. As he walked, Basque removed his mittens and placed them in his coat pocket. He flexed his digits, rubbed his hands together, then fell onto the bench beside Wattle. Basque's red raincoat stood out against the seat's wooden slats.

Wattle shoved his hand into his paper bag, then pulled out a slice of shoulder joint laced with fat. "Don't worry, you didn't miss anything. The meeting's almost over."

Basque scrubbed his eyes. "How many?"

"Eleven." Wattle belched, then jammed the meat into his mouth, chewing around his words. "Three girls this time. The Chato Murciano triplets. You know, the ones who threw rocks at my car."

"Yeah." Basque's wristwatch beeped and he looked up, then grinned at the sturdy teenager trotting towards them from the other side of the street—a cornflower-blue umbrella was clutched tightly in the girl's hand.

Grice shook rain off her umbrella as she neared the bench, then she folded it shut as she fell beside Basque. She slid the umbrella under the seat, then nodded at the Community Centre. "Any news?"

"There's news, but it ain't gucci." Wattle snorted. "Basque's theory has been officially debunked. Destroyed. Shot to Hell."

"We get it." Basque smiled at Grice. A raindrop nestled in one of her dimples. He gently brushed it off her cheek. "You missed one."

"Gag me." Wattle dropped his empty bag on the wet pavement, then shoved his hand into another snack package: this one contained a flaky pastry. "You shouldn't be so cheery. Now that the blanket-brutes have been gone for a week—and six more kiddos are missing—the town is totes cray-cray."

"Six?" Grice leaned around Basque to peer at Wattle. "I thought five more went missing."

"I'm sorry. Were you in the meeting, or was I?" Wattle's grin hardened. "Was I playing in the rain, or were you?"

"There are five more missing kids." Grice's cobalt eyes turned steel grey. "Meishan Mangalica disappeared a few days ago, Pennywell Piétrain's stepbrother was abducted over the weekend and the triplets went missing last night. That's five."

Wattle sneered, then he shrugged and licked salt off his croissant. "Five, six. What difference does it make? Point is, Basque was wrong." He smirked as he sucked on the pastry. "You both were wrong."

Grice sat back, then gnawed her fingernail. "Is the inspector still looking into it?"

"Always." Wattle belched. "She'll tell us what she didn't find tomorrow."

Basque sighed. "Someone has to do something."

"You want the meeting highlights? I stayed for most of it, but left after Loppy Loo started yelling."

Basque nodded. "Please."

Wattle grinned. Bits of buttery bread stuck out of his smile. "Okay, listen up. Today, the popular theories that the town came up with are that the kids drowned swimming-"

"No."

"-or were victims of door violence-"

"Really?"

"-or that the pedos from the Net ripped themselves away from their laptops long enough to specifically target our vulnerable youngsters. Liv calmed them down, but they'll have more suggestions tomorrow."

Basque sighed. "The kidnappings have got to stop." He looked at Wattle, whose porky tongue scythed out of and around his lips. Basque winced. Trying to dismiss the disturbing images conjured by his mind at the sight of Wattle's piggish tongue, Basque thread his fingers through Grice's. She squeezed his hand, then rest her head on his shoulder. Basque smiled down at his crush. His face stayed cool. His smile stayed in place. "Should we go in there?"

Wattle smirked. "Too late. Now."

# CARGO MOVEMENT

## 3

THERE'S NO ROOM TO MOVE, but everyone keeps driving. After we steered into the skid and embraced the holistically vehicular life humanity got what it wanted. We became a societal behavioural pendulum and the new world swung between what we feared and what we needed. Tight proximity. Total connectivity. Technology that fused us together. Permanent, inflexible, unchanging. Squished. Cramped. Close. MY FAMILY WAS ONE OF THE FIRST TO JOIN THE CARGO MOVEMENT. We migrated, transferring into our truck and taking to the road as the government bulldozed our home to make way for the interconnected transcontinental roadway system. My grandmother was one of the architects who designed the oceans' pavement pathways. Her name is synonymous with modern development. Our brand is associated with royalty. I am a Prince. I can't breathe. MY CAR IS SMALL, like most of them are these days. Not like when I was young and our truck fit all five of my family members—and our belongings—with space to spare. When I got my graduated licence at fourteen, chose my driving co-pilot, then moved out and into my own home—my own vehicle, my own car—the government had already passed regulation that wouldn't allow vehicles larger than two-seaters to be manufactured. "Better for the environment," they said. "Easier on the wallet," was the claim. "Nobody wants compartmentalized separation, anyway. We want vehicles to drive side by side. We want vehicles to be parked in lots. We want vehicles to improve spacial relationships. We want vehicles so there's no privacy, no primacy, no personality— so there's no point in us creating larger units anymore. Larger units are a thing of the past. A troubled past, and one we are driving further and further away from, thanks to people like your grandmother. So, our apologies—your majesty—but what you want is no longer possible." WHAT ENVIRONMENT? I said. Nature had been paved over to put up paradise. Green wasn't necessary or viable. All production moved underground. All manufacturing moved underground. All cultivation moved underground. The surface was for driving. The environment was rock and stone and signage and traffic lights. WHAT WALLETS? I said. Currency was obsolete. Everything we needed—from tire repair, to charging stations, to nutrient rations, to driving entertainment—was provided. We have no wallets, because we have no money, because there's nothing we need to beg for. The government provides. Now, we travel, we're united, we belong, we're taken care of—it works. NOBODY WANTS SEPARATION, I thought, alone in my two-seater with my driving partner. After one hundred years of endemic, pandemic and epidemic isolation humanity rejected rejection and shifted to a we-are-one model of interaction. Without homes or offices or theatres, stadiums, playgrounds, arenas—with nothing but cars—we became surrounded in an ever-moving community of humans that co-exist on our global roads, always moving forward as one, passing new caravans every day, our soul-spouse in the passenger seat, the electric systems in our vehicles taking us to our predetermined destinations, the landscape an ever-reaching solid sea of black-cracked concrete and sun-beached road bumpers with metal grates to break up the monotony of our existential expressway ennui, and-

My LIFE FEELS LIKE A CAGE. I'm trapped.
Unable to inhale. WHEN I WAS A CHILD I
literally couldn't inhale because of the air pollution.
Now that we live IN A NUCLEAR, electric, solar
powered world the air is CLEAN AND fresh but my
lungs aren't able to take it in. Everything is tinted
BY THE SCENT of metal. And plastic fixtures. And
neon afterimage. They colour my VISION WITH
permanent sprays of red turn signals, blinking
EXIT SIGNS and buzzing infotisements, telling
me and MY CO-PILOT what meals we'll recieve
that evening and WHO we'll be parked beside
when my two-seater pulls into our assigned LOT-

"CURY," says Saturn, my side-seat driver, my navigation-
specialist, my race-crew, my gearbox-conductor. "Cury,"
says Saturn. "You're staring again." I DON'T TURN
FROM THE WINDOW. Why would I? I know what Saturn
looks like. I know how he's sitting, foot resting on the
dashboard, arm hanging out the window, hand flipping his
aviators—up, shut, clear, shaded. He watches our daily
driveo on our screeneo, a story about the perils of past life.
The heroine is chased through a forest by bees. The hero is

dying under an avalanche slide. The heroix searches through rain, hail, sleet, cyclones, hurricanes, tornadoes, trying to connect, always apart, never reaching the safety of each other's arms. The driveo is a horror story. A reminder of what we're most afraid of. A way to remember what we're hiding from that's safer than talk, safer than feeling, safer than sleep. Safer than memory. I hear the screams of the underground actors filling the car, but my eyes stay outside. SATURN SAYS, more loudly, "You never look at me anymore. Stop staring and wake up. For once." His words are loud but his voice doesn't resonate in the void. He whispers, hisses, wheezes and moans. His words are meant to engage, to hurt, ENRAGE!, but his voice is soft. Demure. Easy to block out. Easy to mute and pretend I'm in here by myself. SATURN'S ARMS ARE THIN AND PALE. Our skin is safe, protected by the windshield's UV glass, even though radiant rays are a non-issue because the ozone repaired itself. Saturn is thin and pale. We all are. Human muscles are no longer needed. Our diet is so strictly monitored we are perfectly balanced unblemished versions of humans, unlike the messy, complex, inconsistent ones that ruined the earth. We are fragile. We get to be precious because our cars act as our legs. As our bodies. Our defences. I'M STARING OUT MY WINDOW BECAUSE THAT'S WHAT I DO. There was a time when royalty had purpose. People like me were more than shallow symbols of progress. Now, all I do is watch the roads ahead of us and behind, the different coloured cars moving by and moving on. We whiz along at a steady pace, never slowing, rarely stopping. I would gladly give up my symbols to leave this life, all my carbon crowns and rubber rings and broaches made of batteries. A car with two small passengers passes us by, the kids laughing at the forested driveo on their screeneo. They've never known forest. How hilarious a tree must seem to them. I STARE OUT THE WINDOW BECAUSE I HAVE SEEN A TREE. The manufactured props on the driveo screeneo are nothing compared to the barky beasts from my childhood. The driveo maples are wilted. The driveo poplars are small. The driveo conifers are thin and pale. Their branches look like Saturn's forearms. Like his thighs, resting on top of his firm, supported, pleather, luxurious interior recliner. I don't need to turn away from my window. I know what Saturn's thighs look like.

the trees from my childhood are wild.

thick, towering and unpredictable. roots clawing out of

the earth. branches reaching towards the heavens.

bark rough, flaking during the hot season and twigs

withering during the cold. budding when it never rains with

tiny, cracked leaves spiralling towards the barren ground

when the winds pick up. the trees from my childhood

shrink every year and are barely taller than my head when

my grandmother leads us out of our house and into our cage.

there is a nest, too. when I am very, very young.

a bird tried to lay

eggs but those were

impossible and

soon she died.

all the birds died.

and the beetles

and the botanicals

and the borers.

the ones that survived moved underground to be protein

facilitators now we eat eggs on holidays the government

includes them in our ration boxes on Merge Day Saturn

eats the eggs i look out the window hoping i'll see a bird

THERE'S NO ROOM TO MOVE, but the cars keep driving. The road stretches ahead of us, black and grey and endless pavement. Saturn watches the driveo on the screeneo and I stare out the window. I stare at the cars and at the faces of the thin, pale, fragile, weak, helpless, heartless, futile, frightened, precious cargo within their frames. Humans are interconnected—protected. We are safe and secure. I stare out the window and watch our lives pass by

we KEEP MOVING FORWARD.

# UNDER A CAT-MUNIST REGIME

# 4

Royal Canuckian Mounted Police pushed Voter into the interrogation room. Voter stumbled in the police officer's grip as he tried to maintain his footing. Royal Canuckian grumbled. They pushed Voter into the metal chair that sat behind the interrogation table, then unlocked Voter's handcuffs. Royal Canuckian grabbed Voter's hands, held them in front of his face and clapped the cuffs around his wrists. The officer grumbled as they attached Voter's handcuffs to a bar that protruded from the table. Voter pulled on his restraints and watched with bemused confusion as Royal Canuckian marched out of the room, gently shutting the door behind them.

The amber-lit hanging lamp swung ominously above Voter's head. He looked around the empty room, quietly laughed, then pulled on his restraints again. Voter fell against the back of the chair and snorted, mildly annoyed. "Alright. Here we go."

The door swung open. A woman with a voluptuous figure swayed into the interrogation room, clasping a beige file folder against her ample chest with one fleshy hand. The other fleshy hand dragged a second chair into the room behind her. She swivelled the seat around to face Voter. She nestled her curvy bottom into the chair and placed the folder on the table. The woman cleared her throat, then spoke in a low raspy voice. "I assume you know why you're here today."

Voter shook his head. "No one told me. I was at home when RCMP broke down my door and dragged me here." He leaned towards the woman. "What's going on? If I did something wrong I can explain, but you have to tell me why I was arrested."

The voluptuous woman ran her fingers over the file folder. "I'm here to help you. I'm Reeve, the representative for your county. Just tell me what I need to know, and you can go home."

"Sure, anything." Voter nodded at his restrained hands. "I'll answer anything. Whatever you need."

"Good." Reeve stroked the folder. "I assume you know why you're here today."

"No, uh—I don't." Voter attempted a half-smile. "I'm sure this is some kind of mistake."

"Just tell us what we need to know, and you can go home."

Voter frowned. "I want to. What do you need to know?"

"Don't play games with me, Voter."

"I'm not playing games." Voter swallowed, then tried another smile. "I'd like to clear up this misunderstanding. But I don't know what the misunderstanding is."

Reeve tapped the folder with her fingernail. "You know what's in here."

"I don't."

"You know what you've been charged with."

"No, I don't."

"You know what you did. What you've been doing for fifteen years." She leaned forward. Her bosom pressed into the table. "Didn't think you'd get caught, did you? But we always find out—eventually."

Voter looked around the interrogation room, his half-smile frozen in place. "We?"

"We know."

"Know what?"

"What you did."

"What did I do?"

Reeve stood. Her chair bumped across the floor. She reached forward, grabbed the edge of the folder, then slowly slid it towards her rounded abdomen. She hugged the beige file to her chest and swayed out of the room.

Voter watched the door close with wide, bewildered eyes. "What in the world?"

The door swung open. A man with stubble on his cheeks stumbled into the room, holding a tablet between his gnarled fingers. He stumbled to the second chair and fell into the seat, his eyes scanning the room's impenetrable walls as he turned to face Voter. He flipped open the tablet and pushed it across the table. Voter stared at the screen as the man cleared his throat and spoke in a gratingly weak voice. "Alright, Friend. Tell me the truth. Why'd you do it?"

Voter tore his eyes away from the screen, blinking at the man. "Do what? This?" He nodded at the tablet, smiling. "Have a Meta account?"

"It's what's on the account, Friend-o. It's what's on it."

Voter squinted. "Who are you?"

"I'm Councillor. Ward Councillor. Don't you recognize me?"

"Oh." Voter tilted his head. "You're always shaved in pictures."

"Exactly." Councillor tapped the tablet with his gnarled fingers. "The pictures, Friendster. Let's talk about the pictures."

"Of you?"

"No, on your Facebook account. Stay with me, Froonstie."

"I don't share pictures on Facebook. I mean, Meta. Just memes."

"Exactly, Frienderino. The memes. That's why you're here. It would be a real shame if something had to happen to you because of the memes."

Voter glanced down at the tablet, then back up at Councillor. "Those memes?"

"Exactly. Who knows what the higher powers would do if they saw these."

"The memes on my Meta page?"

"Fifteen years is a long time to be circulating this kind of stuff. I would hate it if you had to be punished in some way because of it."

"I would hate that, too." Voter wrinkled his nose. "Why am I being punished?"

"The stuff, Friendy-diddy-doodle." Councillor rubbed his stubble. "If I had to tell Member of the Legislative Assembly about this it wouldn't go well for you."

"Wait." Voter lifted his finger. "Please, I need an explanation. You arrested me because for the last fifteen years I've shared cat memes on Facebook?"

"It would be a real shame if the higher-ups had to make an example of you."

"Like—those cat memes?" Voter's lips twitched as he held in a smile. "Grouchy Cat and Terror Tabby?"

"Who knows what will happen if you don't admit to your crime."

"Pictures of cats? Cat pictures with captions?" Voter swallowed to stop a giggle from leaking out his lips. "Like,

Just Keep Looking Cute—They'll Blame the Dog? And, Hovercat to Base—Purrmission to Land?" He grinned. "Those pictures?"

"I would hate it if you had to be an example so other psychos don't follow in your footsteps."

Voter smirked. "Don't you mean, paw-steps?"

Councillor froze. His gnarled fingers shook on his stubbled chin. He glared at Voter, then picked up his tablet, flipping it closed. "A real shame, Friend. A real shame." Councillor stumbled out of the interrogation room.

Voter shook his head, chuckling. "Crazy mother-"

The door swung open. A woman with frizzy hair bounced into the room holding a tin lunchbox in her hand. The word MAYOR was scrawled across its side in black felt-tipped marker. Mayor flopped onto the second chair, opened the lunchbox, then removed a covered tray. She placed the tray on the table and lifted the cover—the platter was filled with neatly stacked lines of sushi, row after row. With a flourish, Mayor removed a set of chopsticks from the lunchbox. She beamed at Voter, then stabbed a piece of the raw fish. She popped the sashimi into her mouth. "Ger."

Voter blinked. "Excuse me?"

Mayor swallowed. "Go."

Voter looked over his shoulder, then back at Mayor. "Go where?"

Mayor started on the next piece of fish.

Voter smiled. "Do you expect me to say something?"

Mayor ripped open a packet of soya sauce and dumped the salty brown liquid on a salmon slice.

Voter chuckled. "I'm not going to say anything."

Mayor popped a piece of white tuna in her mouth.

Voter frowned. "I'm not kidding."

Mayor swallowed the tuna.

Voter grunted. "I won't speak."

Mayor started on the next row.

Voter growled. "You want me to talk?"

Mayor swept her frizzy bangs off her forehead.

Voter rolled his eyes, then glared at amber-lit hanging lamp. "Fine. I'll talk." He leaned towards Mayor. "You want to know why I share cat memes? Because cats are funny. My girlfriend has a cat. He's a calico and his name is Bustopher Jones. You want to know why I've shared cat memes for fifteen years? Because cat memes are harmless.

Sometimes, they spread joy. I'm not a bad person. I don't pick fights on the internet. I don't access adult content. I don't like it when grownups use kids to fulfill their own unachieved dreams. Cat memes make me laugh. They're weird and silly and a perfectly good waste of my time. That's why I share cat memes. Can I leave now?"

Mayor tussled her frizzy hair, packed up her tin lunchbox and left the room without a word.

Voter sighed as the door swung shut.

The door swung open. A man with a chalky complexion drifted into the room and onto the second seat. An ID badge declaring M.L.A. hung on a lanyard around his neck. It swung back and forth as it bumped against his hollowed chest. The chalky man tugged on his lanyard, then cleared his throat. "You are a bad person, Mr. Voter."

Voter snorted. "Tell me how sharing cat memes on social media resulted in this." He pulled on his restraints. "You're Member of the Legislative Assembly? Can you give me some answers?"

"Mr. Voter, I'm not here to give you answers. I'm here to get answers." MLA tugged on his lanyard. "You are accused of spreading conspiratorial lies which resulted in the public anti-government outcries that plagued our country these past ten months. How do you plead, Mr. Voter?"

A laugh bubbled out of Voter's mouth. He bit his lip, then swallowed his snickers. "Okay, you've had your fun." He grinned as he swivelled on his seat, peering up into the corners of the ceiling. "This is a joke, right? Did my girlfriend put you up to this?" He smirked at MLA. "You're a good actor. You guys had me going for a while there."

MLA tugged on his lanyard.

"Wait." Voter frowned. "Are you serious?"

"The government is always serious." MLA wrapped his chalky fingers around his badge. "Taxes don't pay for funny business, Mr. Voter. How do you plead?"

Voter snorted. "Am I on trial?"

"Guilty, then." MLA shoved the laminated badge under his armpit. "You can't deny it. We've already issued a press release detailing your crimes to the public. Several acquaintances have blocked you since this morning."

"You did what?!"

"Where did you get the pictures?" MLA removed the badge from his pit. "Do you have a dealer? Someone who's running the show? Is it a Following? Have you been manipulated? Or catipulated?"

"What?" Voter pulled on his restraints. "No!"

"Then you are the leader of the Following, Mr. Voter." MLA shoved his badge under his other arm. "How did you do it? Subliminal messaging in the memes? Are the cats' eyes code for something? Or the patterns in their fur? Tail length? Claw sharpocity?"

"That's not even a word!"

"Calm down."

"Excuse me?"

"You are overreacting."

"You're accusing me of a ridiculous crime because I shared cat memes on the internet!"

"You need to work on your sensitivity."

"My sensitivity?"

"You can't take things so personally, Mr. Voter."

"Billions of people share cat memes." Voter shook his head, then shook his cuffs. "You need to work on your insanity."

"If you're going to attack me I can't negotiate with you." MLA stood. He wiped his moist badge on his sweater, then straightened it with his chalky hand. "I'm not the villain here, Mr. Voter." He drifted out the door.

Voter struggled in his restraints. He pulled on the handcuffs until his wrists turned red. Voter cursed. "Of all the low down, messed up, pieces of-"

The door swung open. A deep sultry voice said, "Now, now. Profanity doesn't help anyone." A man with a heart-shaped face limped into the room. He removed his smart phone from his blazer pocket and placed it on the table in front of Voter. Clearing his throat, he clicked opened an app, started a recording, then said, "I'm Premier. It's in both our best interests if we do this right."

Voter blinked rapidly and shook his head—trying to remove sweat from his eyes. "Can I get a towel?"

"You piece of shit. Who do you think you are?"

Voter gasped. "Excuse me?"

"Oh, you're playing the fool now? Of course you are, you fool. You're such a moron. You don't have to play the fool—you are the fool!"

"That's—uh-" Voter paled. "That's not really fair-"

"Uh, that's not fair, I'm playing the fool, I'm a moron, blah blah blah." Premier slammed his hand on the table. "Shut your mouth!"

Voter leaned back, eyes wide. Sweat began to drip down the back of his neck. "Look, I just want to get out of here."

Premier laughed. "You look, moron. Listen. I got a great joke for you. How many criminals does it take to get out of government custody?"

"Uh—I, uh-"

"None." Premier slapped his knee. "They never get out of government custody."

Voter swallowed. "Good one?"

"Shut your foolish mouth!" Premier leaned closer. "I'm going to use this recording to prove to the world what a moron you are. After we release this to the press you're going to lose all your acquaintances, your family will hate you, your boss will fire you, your dog will run away, your kids will apply for foster care-"

"Whoa, not cool."

"-your girlfriend will leave you for a hotter, non-criminal criminal-"

"That doesn't make any sense!"

"Don't interrupt me. Your pathetic life is over. You're going to jail for the rest of your life. No one gets away with posting cat memes for fifteen years. No one!" Premier stopped the recording. His phone screen faded to black. He smiled. "That wasn't so hard, was it?"

Voter's stomach flipped. His hands began to shake. "You're crazy."

"Now, now. Insults don't help anyone." Premier slipped his phone into his blazer pocket and his smile broadened, dividing his heart-shaped face in two. "The next Official is much more fun, I promise." He stood, kicked his chair to the far side of the room, then limped into the hallway.

Voter's hands shook in the cuffs. His heart throbbed inside his throat. His eyes stayed locked on the door.

The door swung open. A person with unruly eyebrows careened into the room. They banged into the second seat, hit their knee against the chair's leg, then toppled against the table, knocking it to the side.

"Whoops." They tumbled into the second chair and grabbed the sides of the table, trying to straighten it. Their grabbing pulled Voter up and out of his seat—he was still attached to the metal bar. The person giggled. "Sorry. Forgot about you."

They scooted their chair towards the stabilized table, then gasped. "Shoot! One sec." They careened out of the room and promptly returned, holding a box stamped with the Royal Canuckian insignia. They careened back to their seat and dropped the box on the floor. "Darn it. I'm not supposed to do that."

They bent over, disappearing behind the table, then re-emerged—holding a clunky microphone and speaker in their hands. They fumbled with the technology, squinting out from under their unruly eyebrows as they set it up. After more fumbling and squinting the person poked the assembled mic, then giggled. "That was harder than Allan said it would be."

"Allan?"

"Our tech guy. He's a genius with this stuff. I wanted him to set it up for me, but Monarch didn't want anyone to interfere with—well, you know. Ready to get started?"

"Who are you?"

"Oh! Yeah, that's important. Okay, I'll tell you who I am and then we'll get started. Sound good?"

Voter sighed. "Fine."

"Excellent. Great! So, I am Member of Parliament. Happy to meet you."

"Uh huh."

MP giggled. They scratched the side of their nose and their wrist brushed up against their unruly eyebrows, forcing the hairs to stand straight up. "Okay. For reals now. Let's get started." Their grin slid into a seductive smirk. They pressed their lips against the microphone and purred. "Alright, big boy. Why'd ya do it?"

Voter sat up. "Sorry?"

"Mmm. Tough guy, eh?" MP ran their tongue along the microphone's steel tube. "Big boy wants to play? I like to play."

Voter sighed, then dropped his chin to his chest. "I just want to go home."

"Home, eh? Yeah, you like it at home." MP breathed into the mic. A sultry sigh poured out of the speaker. "Alright, baby. Let's get you home. Tell Member of Parliament why you posted the kitties and I'll clean your whiskers."

Voter stared at the table.

MP opened the top button of their shirt—their chest swelled, freshly oiled and glistening in the light from the hanging lamp. "Come on, baby. I'm curious. You don't want my curiosity to kill me, do you?" They unclasped another button. "Do you? Big boy?"

Voter stared at his cuffs.

"Your cattitude has landed you in some toxic litter. Help me clean it out. Tell me why you-" MP leaned back in the chair and opened their legs. "-spread the fur-fetched lies."

Voter stared at the ceiling.

MP laughed, low and heavy, then licked their lips as they arched their back and moaned. "Mmm, I like a man who's hard to comb." They leaned over the table, then ran their fingers across its surface and onto Voter's chained hands. They tickled Voter's fingers and pouted. "Is that a dead mouse on your lap or are you just happy to see me?"

Voter thought about hanging chads.

"I'm just kitten around." MP stroked their unruly brows. "Spill the saucer and give me the-"

"Stop!" Voter shook his head. "What do you want from me? I didn't do anything wrong. I want to go home."

"You're pulling my wool, Catnip." MP chewed their bottom lip, then slid their finger in-between Voter's cuff and wrist, then out. In, then out. In, then out. "Tell me the truth. What do you have against Canuckians?"

Voter wrenched his hands away from MP. "Nothing!"

"Sweetie, baby, you're trying the last of my nine lives." MP's finger slid up Voter's wrist, then eased towards his elbow. "You might be able to spot a bird from across the yard, but I can smell a rat."

Voter closed his eyes. He tried to ignore the tremors running up his legs. "Stop." He shivered. "Just—send in the next one."

MP rumbled, low in their throat. They stretched their arms languorously over their head. Then, with swift proficiency, MP swiped the microphone and speaker off the table and into the box, then climbed out of their seat and loped towards the door. "Purrfect."

The door swung open. Three men dressed in identical navy pinstripe suits marched into the room. They stood behind the table in a clean, crisp line and watched Voter through bulbous eyes.

Voter cleared his throat. "And you are?"

"Minister of Defence. Cyber Security Division."

"Minister of Agriculture. Feline Division."

"Minister of Health. Psychedelic Medicine Division."

"Pleased to meet you. I'm Minister of Voting. You Can Suck It Division."

The three Ministers stared. Their bulbous eyes lit up, then fell into shadow as the amber-lit hanging lamp swung back and forth over Voter's head. The three Minsters cleared their throats in unison, then struck.

"Why did you choose the profile name Voter Fraudisfun?"

"How many cats do you own?"

"Would you say you suffer from depression?"

"Who sold you the meme creation software?"

"What do you do with the cats after you're finished taking pictures of them?"

"Would you say you suffer from anxiety?"

"When does your Meta cult meet to plan the protests?"

"Where do you bury the cats after they've died for your cause?"

"Would you say you suffer from borderline narcissistic bipolar schizophrenic hyper-reactive attention deficit mood disorder or are you just looking for attention?"

The amber-lit hanging lamp swung back and forth over Voter's head. He counted to three, then took a deep breath. "I was twelve when I created my account. None. No. I don't create memes. I don't take pictures of cats. No. There is no cult, at least not one that I organize or follow. No cats have died near, by, or around me, ever. And—finally!—no, absolutely not, eat my excrement, loosen your ties and pick on someone who's undecided."

The three Ministers blinked their bulbous eyes, then marched from the room. Voter leaned back in his chair and counted to ten.

The door swung open. The Prime Minister of Canuckia strolled into the room. She flipped her waist-length fishtail braid over her shoulder as she cradled her mug of tea against her breasts. Without slowing, she strolled over to Voter and threw the hot tea in his face.

"Ahhh!"

Prime Minister broke the empty mug over Voter's head. He ducked down, shaking shards of ceramic out of his hair. Prime Minister raised her hand and slapped Voter's cheek.

"Ow!"

Prime Minister kicked him in the shins.

"Stop it!"

Prime Minster backhanded him across his jaw.

"You bitc-"

Prime Minister kneed him in the groin.

"Oof!"

Prime Minister raised her elbow and slammed it down on the back of his neck.

"Fucking hel-"

Prime Minister grabbed his chin, then forced it upwards so Voter stared into her eyes. He winced. "I'm sorry, I'm sorry, I'm so-"

Prime Minister spit in his face.

Voter squeezed his eyes shut, crying.

Prime Minister strolled behind his chair, then wrapped her long fishtail braid around Voter's neck. He gasped for breath. She pulled her braid tighter. He writhed and contorted. Prime Minister released her chokehold, swatted the back of Voter's head with the end of her braid, then strolled out the door. Voter fell onto the table. He bent over his cuffed hands—gasping—then collapsed. Blood ran into his eyes from the cuts in his scalp. Voter wept onto his arms.

The door stayed shut. The hanging lamp swung above Voter's head. Voter lay still; forehead resting on his wrists, breath wheezing out of his mouth, pulse shallow and weak. Exhaustion rolled over his body in waves.

No one came into the room.

The door swung open.

Monarch walked into the interrogation room.

She crossed her arms over her chest and leaned against one of the impenetrable walls. Monarch looked down at Voter, then smiled. "How would you feel if we were to have a proper conversation?"

Voter looked up from the table. His hands trembled, smeared with the blood from his head. His tears soaked the collar of his once-blue shirt. He sniffed, then lowered his eyes. "I would feel good about it. Madam."

Monarch walked over to the table, then patted Voter's cuffed hands. "There's a good lad." She leaned against her wall. "Now. Would you like me to tell you why you're here?"

"Yes, please."

"Very good lad." Monarch smiled. "You are here because Intelligence told me that cat memes are a form of public manipulation, your attempt to become a national Influencer so you can gradually integrate harmful content onto your feed and turn the voting population against their protective governing body." She crossed her arms. "Does that sound like the truth?"

"Yes, madam."

"Are you willing to sign a written confession attesting to that?"

"Yes, madam."

"Are you willing to verbally admit to your crime before the judicial court?"

"*Oui, madame.*"

"Are you willing to attend government-facilitated rehab for two years—at your personal expense—before returning peacefully to public life?"

"enh, ogimaakwe"

"I'd prefer if you'd communicate in one of the recognized languages, lad."

Voter looked up. "*Oui, madame. Tout ce que vous voulez, Madame. Cela vous suffit-il, madame?*"

"Yes, lad. More than good enough." Monarch uncrossed her arms, pushed herself away from the wall, then cleared her throat. "Next time, think before you *chat*, eh?"

# OH MY GOD, I LOVE THAT FIGUREHEAD

# 5

I was the Tea Carrier that day.

Usually, Amica had the honour of carrying the leaves, but she was sick. Something to do with too much sunlight— heat stroke, or something like it. Amica was a dedicated harvester, the top in our county, and she was often ill because she over-extended herself. So, that day, I was the person responsible for the leaves. For their bagging and plunking, dipping and swirling. I had to ensure that every member of our book club had their water temperature perfect—180 degrees—and that the steep time was optimized for the chosen blend.

Amica chose the blend. She made a list, weeks in advance, of what tea would be served for which book on which date. She selected the leaf based on the season, the events happening in the county throughout the year and the theme of the book we were reading. If I had to choose the blend, I would choose wrong. Like the time I served the lavender the same week Tetley Swivel got married. I'm still haunted by the memory of her devastated face.

That day, we were reading *Ode to a Flower Blossom,* it was springtime and Sencha Ignition's baby shower was that weekend—so, of course, Amica chose the ginger.

I carried it in my shaking hands as I walked up the dusty lane that led to the barn where we held our weekly gatherings. The ginger was locked in its wooden box, airtight and well-oiled, preserving the delicate fumes in the pungent leaves so we could best capture their flavour in the tea. I stepped through the gate, then tripped. I gasped. If I dropped the box and it broke it meant the stocks for sure and I still had bruises on my neck from last winter—but, fortunately, the box didn't slip from my fingers. It didn't crack on the hay-strewn gravel, spilling its contents to be plucked up and carried away by the merciless wind. The ginger was safe. Thank Da-Hong-Pao.

Taking a breath I continued up the path, keeping my eyes on the ground ahead of me. The barn door opened and the ceremonial tea bells rang in their rafter brackets. The lights dimmed as I carried the ginger into the barn.

Everyone was there. I was the last. The tea was always brought in last.

Lipton struck the sipping chimes and I placed the box of leaves on the tea table. She leaned towards me as I bent over, then whispered in my ear, "I brought the kettle. It's the maroon one, over by the window."

I turned. A deep burgundy pot of water boiled merrily on the stove. I smiled at Lipton. "You saved me. My new one isn't being delivered until next week."

Lipton shook her blonde head, then grinned as steam slowly filled the barn. "Bad luck about your kettle, but I'm always here to help."

As she turned to gather the china cups she brushed my back with her long, elegant fingers. Shivers ran up my spine. Lipton dared too much, but I loved her adventurous spirit. No other woman had the audacity to touch their Other during a tea ceremony.

I would thank her later.

Lipton brought over the cups and I opened the lid of the box. A collective gasp resonated in the barn as the ginger revealed its sensuous self. The members of the book club broke into applause and I beamed—the leaves were bright, crisp, and their aroma was overwhelming. I had done well.

"What are those?"

The voice broke through the atmosphere like a car horn in the night—harsh, honky and awfully inappropriate.

Lipton paused her water pouring to glare at the man lounging against the door. "Excuse me?"

"I've never seen ones like those before." The man strode into the barn, grinning and extending his hand. "My apologies, ladies. I'm Joe Sayl from the next county over. I know I'm late, but I had a little tractor trouble. That hill's a doozy. Hope I didn't disturb?"

"We're in the middle of the pouring."

"Yes, I can see that. And a grand pouring it is. What leaves are you using?"

My hands started to shake. If I wasn't careful, I'd crush the finer buds and we wouldn't have enough for service that day. This man could ruin everything. I tried desperately to control my voice. "Sir, please. The ritual is almost complete. If you'll take your seat?"

Sencha—Da-Hong-Pao bless her—appeared at the man's elbow. She steered him towards the nearest cushion.

The man blinked in amusement at the portly girl who had his arm locked in a pincer-like grip. "Alright, no need to pull. I'll hold my tongue 'til it's tea time."

I nodded my head graciously—benevolently—as Sencha guided the man to his cushion. Breathing in deeply, Lipton and I finished the Pouring and placed each china cup on the serving tray. Tetley did her duty by walking through the cushions, grasping the tray firmly in both hands. Her wedding ring flashed in the light from the candles. Each member of the club bowed before selecting their cup.

The man chuckled, then swirled his brew before inhaling its fumes with religious fervour. "Say what you will about country folk, but you sure steep the nicest tea in the district. My thanks." And without waiting for the rest of us—without following the ritual—the man took a swig from his cup and smacked his lips. "Delicious." He downed the tea to its leaves and held his cup out for more. "If you'd be so obliged?"

I stared at him, horrified. Lipton's jaw dropped. Tetley whimpered softly, clutching the empty tray. Sencha cradled her baby in her arms and murmured soothing words into her ear.

The man gazed at us, his hand frozen out in front of him, then he shrugged and tossed the soggy leaves on the ground. He slid off his cushion and stood. "No matter, I can steep my own. Anything left in that box of yours?"

I felt the hair on my arms rise. Lipton gnashed her teeth. The tray fell to the ground as Tetley leaned over a hay bale and vomited into the straw, holding her belly as she retched. Sencha scrambled to her feet, clutching her baby—and the bag containing the copies of *Ode to a Flower Blossom*— tightly against her chest. She ran out of the barn, hitting her shoulder against the wooden doorframe as she went.

The man smiled, then strolled over to the tea table. I couldn't move, I could stop him. He reached out his hand, placed his calloused claws on the pot handle and-

"That's enough of that."

A rolling voice, rich and warm, halted the man's blasphemous activity. Amica walked into the barn, sun at her back, and placed her weather-worn fingers on the man's shoulder. "You should put that pot down, darlin'."

The man grinned at Amica through his crooked teeth, then he dropped his hand.

Thank Da-Hong-Pao, he dropped his hand.

"Are you the lady I spoke with on the phone?" The man leaned closer to Amica, but he didn't bother lowering his voice. "These women are fussed. Maybe you can straighten them out."

"I would love nothing more than to put right the wrongs that have been done here today." Amica's fingers hovered over the man's forearm before grasping his bicep. She guided him towards the cattle shed, back where the tools were kept. "Camellia? You brought the leaves, didn't you? Could you help in the back?"

I swallowed, then nodded, keeping my eyes locked on Amica's. Her gaze was steady. It gave me strength.

"Ladies, please finish your tea." Amica turned to Tetley and smiled, gently. "Can you get after Sencha? How can we discuss our stories if we don't have any books?"

Tetley wiped her mouth, then sprinted down the lane.

Lipton grabbed the hem of my cardigan. She whispered, "You'll be fine. Do it quickly and then we can finish. We have purifiers at home."

I nodded again, then walked close to Amica as she steered the man towards the tool shed.

Amica was all gracious smiles. "My apologies for this break in ritual, but I'm sure you see it's necessary."

The man smirked, his crooked teeth sinister. He fondled his belt buckle as he stepped into the shed. "Never thought these things were that important. I know you take Da-Hong-Pao seriously, and I respect a gal with him in her heart, but I believe that a little moderation in everything is the way to-"

The spade hit the side of the man's skull with a dull *thud!* His ignorant expression held a second—half a second—before his features went slack and he fell to the ground, face first in the dirt.

I dropped the spade on the ground, then wiped my sweating palms on my trousers.

Amica leaned over the body to brush a strand of hair from my eyes. "Good girl. The first one's always hardest." She kicked the body lying at her feet, then shook her head. "I'll ask Yerba to bury the corpse tomorrow. He'll be so disappointed this week's reading got ruined. He loved *Ode* and was excited to talk with you about it at Sencha's shower." She sighed, then held out her hand. "Come, darlin'. We can brew another pot. Best to start these things from the beginning. Da-Hong-Pao won't mind."

I exhaled, relaxing, and tucked my hand safely in Amica's. She led me back into the barn.

"Ladies?" The afternoon sunlight landed on Amica's shoulders, illuminating her steady presence with a holy glow. "Camellia brought the tea today. Let us show her our respect by worshiping the offering of the leaves she's bestowed. Praise Da-Hong-Pao."

Praise Da-Hong-Pao.


I was the Workout Host that day. Usually, Flex hosted the workouts at his apartment, but he was sick. Too much exertion. High blood pressure, or something. Flex was a dedicated spinner, the top runner in our pod, and he got sick a lot because he over-exercised himself. So, that day, I got to host the workout. I got to lead the pod warm-up, wash the foam mats for the recovery cool down, make sure every member of our spin class had their water bottles filled—two litres—and the playlist was loud and bumping.

Flex put together the playlist. He had a Spotify account, bought years ago, and the music was downloaded hours before each spin. He picked the songs based on the trends, the parties going on in our group and the type of workout we were doing. If I had to choose the tunes, I would choose wrong. Like when I played *Daffodils* by Mark Ronson the same week Eschelon Swivel's dog got hit by that car. I still have nightmares about it.

That week, retro music was viral, it was summer and Keiser Ignition was having his bachelor party that weekend—so, of course, Flex chose *Hits from the 20s*.

I pressed the play button with my shaking hand as my friends pushed open my apartment door and busted into the workout room. The playlist was on my laptop, fully charged and hooked up to Alexa so she could run the volume for us. I rifled through my exercise bag, searching for the power cord—but it was missing. I felt sweat start to soak the back of my lycra tank. If I couldn't find the cord, the laptop battery would die and the music would cut out in the middle of the spin. If the workout got ruined, I'd be ghosted from the pod for weeks and I still had on the five pounds I'd gained when I'd been eliminated that spring. Fortunately, I found the cord underneath my trainers. The music would play. Thank Peloton.

I plugged the cord into the nearest wall socket as my buddies threw their bags on my couch. The apartment door closed and the warm-up tunes spilled out from the speakers. I cranked up the volume, then let Alexa take over. Everyone was mounted on their bikes. I was the last. The host always mounted last.

Nordic chugged his water as I tossed him a towel. He leaned towards me, yelling in my ear, "I brought the protein bars! They're in the box by your TV!"

I turned. The bright orange package balanced cheerily against my wireless router. I smiled at Nordic. "You saved me. The grocery store stopped doing deliveries this week."

Nordic shook his shaved head, then grinned as the smell of sweat slowly filled the apartment. "Bad luck about your bars, but I'm always here to help."

As he reached for the towel he brushed the back of my hand with his strong, slick fingers. Shivers ran down my spine. Nordic crossed the line, but I loved his fearlessness. No other guy touched their Bro during a workout.

I would thank him later.

Nordic tossed the towel back, and I yelled, "Let's go harder!" A collective groan rumbled in the apartment as the music ramped up and we peddled faster. The pod sweat on their cycles and I grinned—the workout was brisk, challenging and a calorie burner. I had killed it.

"Did you start without me?"

The voice wrecked our vibes like a whistle in a gymnasium—shrill, piercing and annoying.

Nordic slowed his peddling to glare at the girl who was leaning against the door. "What's up?"

"Vuori said you were starting at seven." The girl skipped into the room, cackling as she waved her hand. "Hey! I'm Joey Sayl, Vuori's next door neighbour. I thought I was going to be early, but I guess I got the time wrong. Can I take the extra bike?"

"We're in the middle of the climb."

"Yeah, I can see that. You look hot. What tension setting are you using?"

My legs started to shake. If I wasn't careful I'd slip out of my peddles and wouldn't be able to lead. This girl could ruin everything. I tried to breathe, sucking in air through my nose. "Look, Joey, we're in the middle of the workout. Take the bike in the corner."

Keiser—Peloton bless him—hopped off his bike and grabbed the girl's elbow. He steered her towards the empty cycle.

Joey cackled at the hefty dude who had her arm loosely pinned to her side. "You don't have to push. Boundaries much? I can climb on myself."

I nodded my head, relieved—exhausted—as Keiser left Joey to her bike. Breathing in deeply, I finished leading the First Climb, shouting out encouragements to the rest of the pod. Eschelon swung off his cycle to refill our waters. He loped into the attached kitchenette and returned with the bottles grasped in both hands. Each member of the pod nodded as he handed them the filled plastic cylinders.

Joey cackled, then swirled her water before taking a gulp with religious fervour. "Say what you will about city guys, but this workout is tight. Thanks for the invite." And without waiting for the rest of us—without following the ritual—Joey climbed off her bike and grabbed a power bar from the box. She ripped open the wrapper and took a bite. "So good." She stuffed the rest of the bar in her mouth, then reached for another. Joey held up the box and shook it— empty. "Got any more?"

I stared at her, horrified. Nordic's hand slipped off his handle. Eschelon gasped, holding his water bottle to his chest. Keiser stared resolutely at the screen on his stationary, pretending not to see this atrocious behaviour.

The girl gazed at us, her hand holding the empty box upside down, then she shrugged and tossed it on the floor. "Whatever. I can find them. I'll go through your stuff. Anything I can grab for you?"

I felt the hair on my arms rise. Nordic ground his teeth. Eschelon's bottle fell to the kitchen tiles as he leaned over the sink and puked into the basin, holding his topknot back as he barfed. Keiser leapt off his bike, clutching his workout bag in one hand and struggling into his cool down gear with the other. He ran out of the apartment, hitting his shoulder against the aluminum doorframe as he went.

Joey rolled her eyes, then skipped over to the couch. I couldn't move. I couldn't stop her. She reached out her hand, placed her manicured talons on my bag strap, ripped open the velcro and-

"That doesn't belong to you."

A clear voice, high and cold, stopped the girl's blasphemous activity. Flex walked into the apartment and

the musty outside air billowed in behind him. I shivered as he placed his tanned fingers on Joey's thin shoulder. "Have we met?"

Joey turned to Flex and her crooked lips peeled back. She removed her hand from my bag strap.

Thank Peloton, she removed her hand from my bag strap.

"You were at the bar last night. With Vuori." Joey leaned closer to Flex, but kept shouting over the music. "I actually wanted to get to know you better! Can you show me how to get my sweat on?"

"That is definitely something I can do." Flex chuffed the girl's chin, then led her towards the spare bedroom—back where the extra equipment was kept. "Vuori? You're leading the workout, right? Can you show us the free weights?"

I swallowed, then nodded, keeping my eyes locked on Flex's. His gaze was steady. It gave me strength.

"Hey, guys? Finish the spin." Flex turned to Eschelon. "Can you get Keiser? The workout isn't the same unless the whole pod is here."

Eschelon spit into the sink, then ambled out the door.

Nordic helped me climb off my bike, giving my shoulder a squeeze. "You'll be fine. Do it quickly and then we can finish. I have sanitizer at my place."

I nodded again, then hurried after Flex as he led Joey to the spare bedroom.

He was all smiles. "Hopefully this will make up for us not hanging out last night."

Joey smirked, her crooked lips repulsive, and she fluttered her small hand against her chest as she stepped into the bedroom. "I don't get why you guys take these workouts so seriously. I know Peloton is important and everything, and dudes are sexy when they respect the Lord, but I don't understand why you invest so much time into-"

The dumbbell smashed the back of the girl's head with a *squelch!* Her idiotic expression held a second—half a second—before her eyes went dim and she fell onto the bed, face first into a pillow.

I placed the dumbbell on the floor, then wiped my sweating palms on my track pants.

Flex lightly punched my shoulder. "Good work. The first one's always hardest." He rolled the body onto its back, then shook his head. "I'll DM Níkē—she can clean this up tomorrow." Flex sighed. "She'll be so pissed the workout got ruined. She wanted to know your time so she could beat you next week." He closed the bedroom door. "It's all good, man. We can order more bars online. Let's just do our cool down and call it. Peloton won't mind."

I took a breath, then followed Flex back into the workout room.

"Pod?" The late-afternoon sunlight landed on Flex's shoulders, illuminating his steady presence with a holy glow. "Vuori led the workout today. Let's show him our kudos by worshiping the awesomeness of the snackage he's bestowed. Praise Peloton."

Praise Peloton.


I was the Office Chair Back Support Adjuster that day.

Usually, Mx. Lumbar had the honour of manually adjusting the seat backs, but they were sick. Something to do with too much photocopying—a paper cut, maybe. Mx. Lumbar was a dedicated admin assistant, the top within the recruiting pool, and they were sickly because they over-worked themself. So, that day, I was the person responsible for the alignments. For the pulling and tweaking, the oiling of the wheels and plumping of the padding. I had to make sure that every employee in the office had a chair that turned in a full circle—360 degrees—and the gears wouldn't squeak when the staff stood up.

Mx. Lumbar trained me. They wrote out the instructions, then emailed me the PDF with maintenance details for every brand. They made repair recommendations in the margins based on employee weight, height and ergonomically-specific support preference. If I made the adjustments without their instructions I would do it wrong. Like when I raised Mrs. Swivel's Tempurpedic two inches too high and she had a crick in her neck from looking down at her desk. I still beat myself up about it.

That morning, there were three employees in the office, a temp on the way and everyone scheduled used the same kind of chair (the Herman Miller Embody, retail price $12,995), so Mx. Lumbar emailed me the Miller manual. Of course.

I held the printed sheets in my shaking hands as I rode the elevator up the thirteen stories to the floor where the office was located. The instructions were in a binder, hole-punched and tucked safely inside plastic sheets so I could easily read the directions. The last time I adjusted the back supports I almost wrecked the page that showed how to tighten the bolts that held the easy glide bumpers in place. I would have lost my administrator licence—I was still paying the reinstatement fees from my previous demotion. Fortunately, that day, the binder didn't pop open, didn't crack upon on the floor of the hardwood hallway, didn't spill the Ancient Forest Protected papers to be snatched up and recycled by the office janitorial staff. The manual was safe. Thank Stumpf.

As the elevator arrived at the thirteenth floor I held the binder close and kept my eyes on the office door, a magnificent blue-tinted glass entranceway. It opened and the ceremonial phones jangled on their power bases. The vertical blinds closed as I carried the manual into the meeting room. I was the last. The manual was always brought in last.

Mr. Caster wheeled four chairs into the room as I placed the manual on the boss' desk. Mr. Caster leaned towards me, hissing in my ear, "I got your message. You won't have to sit down today."

I turned. A medical note was clasped tightly in his hand, signed by my doctor and briefly outlining my back injury. I smiled at Mr. Caster. "Thank you. I'm so embarrassed I can't test the alignments myself."

Mr. Caster grinned as he lined up the chairs perpendicular to the desk. "I'm always here to help."

As he rolled the chairs into a tighter line he brushed my hip with his rough, calloused fingers. Shivers ran across my spine. Mr. Caster took chances, but I loved the risk of an office romance. No other colleague had the courage to touch their Lover during a chair adjustment.

I would thank him later.

I opened the binder. A collective moan rang out in the meeting room as the manual revealed its sharp Times New Roman font. The employees cheered and I beamed—the pages were cream-coloured, straight-edged and there were no rips in the corners. I had done well.

"Am I late?"

The voice resounded in the meeting room like a dial-up taking a fax—loud, nasal and completely unnecessary.

Mr. Caster stepped back from the chairs to glare at the male who was standing by the blue-tinted glass entranceway. "Do you have an appointment?"

"Whoa, your seats are nice." The male strolled into the office, grinning and extending his hand. "I'm Jose Sayl, the temp filling in for Cosm Lumbar today. I hope I'm not interrupting, but the bus ran late. New driver. Anything I can do to jump in?"

"We're in the middle of the alignment."

"Oh, shit. Sorry. Can I help? I do the alignment for my family. My pop's hopeless with a screwdriver."

My hands started to shake. If I wasn't careful I'd crush the thinner pages and wouldn't be able to read the instructions. I desperately tried to control my voice. "I'm comfortable leading the ritual. Why don't you grab a coffee in the break room."

Miss Ignition—Stumpf bless her—appeared at Mr. Sayl's elbow. She steered him towards the common area.

Mr. Sayl blinked in amusement at the statuesque woman who had his arm locked in a clamp-like stronghold. "I can go myself. Just show me the milk powder and I'll be out of your hair."

I nodded my head calmly—patiently—as Miss Ignition guided Mr. Sayl away. Breathing in deeply, Mr. Caster finished lining up the chairs and I knelt down to perform the Straightening. Mrs. Swivel did her duty and brought over the oil, holding the canister in her hand. She patted the top of her Tempurpedic fondly as she walked past it. Each employee stood silently as I focused on the seats.

Mr. Sayl reappeared, sipping from a styrofoam cup as he strolled into the meeting room with sacrilegious audacity. "I temp at a lot of places, but this is the first time I've seen an alignment taken so seriously. It's refreshing." And without asking permission—without following the ritual—Mr. Sayl strolled over to Mrs. Swivel's Tempurpedic and stroked the armrest. "Nice." He plopped down on the seat and spun in a circle, lifting his legs and laughing. "Wow! They give you top of the line, here!"

I stared at him, horrified. Mr. Caster's pen fell out of his hand. Mrs. Swivel whimpered softly and the oil canister trembled. Miss Ignition reached for the phone, then dialled the emergency number with swift efficiency.

Mr. Sayl watched us, his legs frozen out in front of him, then he shrugged and tucked his feet up onto the chair, crossing his legs. "If you're finished I'd appreciate it if someone could push me to Lumbar's desk. They had a to-do list longer than my-" He grinned. "Longer than my you-know-what. Roll me over?"

I felt the hair on my arms rise. The canister fell to the floor as Mrs. Swivel ran into the washroom. I could hear her throwing up in a stall, flushing the toilet as she heaved. Miss Ignition slammed the phone onto its base, then grabbed her briefcase and clutched her purse against her chest. She ran out of the office, hitting her shoulder against the glass doorframe as she went.

Mr. Sayl laughed, then scooted over to the desk, still sitting in the chair. I couldn't move, I couldn't stop him. He reached out his hand, placed his hooks on the easy glide bumper and-

"You know we're in billable hours, don't you?"

A brassy voice, bold and powerful, halted Mr. Sayl's blasphemous activity. Mx. Lumbar walked past the janitor polishing the hardwood in the hallway and into the office. They placed their typist fingers on the back of Mr. Sayl's neck. "Looks like we didn't need you to come in today."

Mr. Sayl grinned at Mx. Lumbar. His white teeth gleamed. He dropped his hand in his lap.

Thank Stumpf, he dropped his hand in his lap.

"You sure you don't need me to pick up the slack?" Mr. Sayl climbed to his feet. "These people are so slow. They take way too long to do a simple adjustment."

"As much as I enjoy helping out temps when I can, there's nothing for you to do today." Mx. Lumbar moved their fingers to Mr. Sayl's lower back and guided him towards the door. Their face looked pinched. "Ms. Avery? You were in charge of the adjustment, weren't you? As soon as our guest leaves, you can continue."

I swallowed, keeping my eyes locked on Mx. Lumbar's. My heart thudded in my chest.

Mx. Lumbar turned to Mrs. Swivel, who was still on her knees as she peered around the washroom door. "There's more oil in the supply closet. Mr. Caster, can you please contact Miss Ignition? I'm sure she'd like to clock her full day."

Mr. Caster gave a smile that didn't reach his eyes, then pulled his cell from his back pocket. He whispered to me as he scanned his screen. "You'll be fine. Try to remain calm and the alignment will go great. We can relax, later."

I nodded, then watched Mx. Lumbar lead Mr. Sayl towards the hallway. "My apologies for the inconvenience. I'll call your recruiter so you can pick up another half day."

"I hope I didn't overstep." Mr. Sayl gently removed Mx. Lumbar's fingers from his back. "I haven't been a temp that long and I really want to do a good job. My oma's ill and my little sister wants to go to summer camp, so if there's any work you can get me I'd really appreciate it."

Mx. Lumbar froze—then seemed to melt. They smiled. "You sound like a go-getter. I'm sorry you've fallen on hard times, but we really are set for the day." They tapped their chin, then looked Mr. Sayl up and down appraisingly. "If you want to be successful at your next contract would you like some advice?"

Mr. Sayl leaned forward, eyes lighting up. "Please. That would be great."

Mx. Lumbar nodded. "Alright. Here's my advice. Review the holy manual about chair maintenance. Our branch takes our figureheads very seriously, so if you want to make it in the high-powered world of finance I recommend you honour the words of his Lord and Saviour, Eugene Stumpf. That is the surest path to achievement."

"I have the holy manual at home." Mr. Sayl smiled. "Gene was a good person."

"Here." Mx. Lumbar reached into their suit jacket pocket and removed a book—clean, pristine, practically glowing. They pressed it into Mr. Sayl's hands. "Take this copy. It's the latest edition. There's a foreword by the prophet Mobius. You'll love it."

"Wow. Thanks!"

"I'll call you the next time we have an opening." Mx. Lumbar placed their hand on the blue-tinted glass doorframe. "Next time."

"Appreciate it." Mr. Sayl slid the manual inside his own jacket pocket, then smirked. His white teeth glistened. He waved his hand over his shoulder. "You know my number." He strolled over the door's threshold and into the hallway. I could hear him whistle a jaunty tune as he headed for the elevators.

The floor polisher cracked his skull with a sickly *crunch!* Through the glass I watched his body hover for a second—half a second—before it went slack and fell to the ground, face first on the hardwood.

The janitor leaned the polisher against the wall, then stepped over the body. He shoved his whiskered face into the office. "I'll have this cleaned up in no time. Thank Miss Ignition for calling. It's always better when a professional takes care of these types."

Mx. Lumbar sneered. "Much obliged. I'll make sure to tell your manager you were supremely helpful."

The janitor grinned, stepped back, then dragged the body up the hallway until we couldn't see it any longer.

Mx. Lumbar sighed, tapped their chin, then nodded at me. "Ms. Avery, I still trust you to perform the ritual today. But start from the beginning. Stumpf would seek retribution if we miss a single step."

I raised the corners of my mouth, trying to show Mx. Lumbar my devotion, but my hands shook as I stepped aside. Sweat beaded on Mr. Caster's brow as he grabbed the wayward chair and rolled it back into the lineup.

"Miss Ignition?" The early-morning sunlight landed on Mx. Lumbar's shoulders, illuminating their sinister presence with an ominous glow. They held the phone against their ear. "You have five minutes. If you're not back here in time for the adjustment you'll be out of a job and I'll send you to Stumpf myself." They hung up the phone, then turned. Mx. Lumbar's eyes glittered as they stared at me and rest of the staff.

We knelt on the floor in front of the chairs. Bowing our heads and lowering our eyes we murmured, as though we were one, "Praise Stumpf."

Mx. Lumbar's voice soared above the sound of the floor polisher revving in the hallway. "Praise Stumpf."

# PAULA IS DEAD

# 6

## MCTRUCKNEY DEAD,

## SUBBED BY SECRET GUITARIST

IG @VCHS by @klein_truthlovepeace

"What the-?" Johanna stared at her screen. She looked over at Georgette, then aimed her phone at the bass guitarist. "Did you see this post?"

"Huh?" Georgette, intent on tuning her instrument, ignored the device being shoved in her face. "What?"

"This post." Johanna shook her phone. "About Paula. Did you see it?"

"Huh?"

"Richie!" Johanna stood. The keyboard resting on her lap hit the gymnasium floor with a *bang!* "Richie, open Insta!"

A voice called from the basketball storage closet. "On it."

"Did you see what the school posted this morning?"

"No."

"Look at the school's feed. Klein the Creep did it again."

Georgette looked up. She squinted her foggy eyes. "Huh?"

"Klein. The school's star reporter. Come on, Georgette. You know who I'm talking about. Klein released another one of her exposés." Johanna crouched beside Georgette and waved her phone at the bassist. "Read it."

Georgette took the phone. Her eyes widened, guitar-tuning forgotten. "What the-?"

## SCHOOL BAND 'SLUG' THROUGH SETS
IG @VCHS by @klein_truthlovepeace


Johanna, Georgette and Richie huddled beside Richie's drum kit. Richie tapped her drumstick against her thigh as she scanned the series of posts shared that morning. "What does this headline even mean?"

"Klein's trying to sound smart." Johanna's fingers twitched as she scrolled on her phone. "But she's a creep."

"I don't get it." Richie sighed. "I thought we played fine."

"We do play fine. Klein is jealous. And a liar." Johanna scratched the side of her neck, glaring at her screen. "Look—this post says Paula's dead, this one says we've been covering it up all year and this one says our replacement singer's a doubleB. None of this is true."

"You sure?" Georgette blinked. "Paula wasn't in Math today."

"Keep calm." Richie twirled her drumstick between her fingers. "I texted Paula. She's sick so she skipped, but she's coming here now."

"You sure?" Georgette squinted. "What if it isn't Paula?"

"Stop it." Johanna looked up. "Paula isn't dead. These rumours are creepy."

Richie pointed her stick at Johanna. "Didn't the school account lose a bunch of followers this week?"

"Yes!" Georgette jumped as Johanna clapped her hands together. "Listen to Richie! Klein's posting these to get more hits."

"The socials are really important to Mrs. Gibb." Richie twirled her stick. "If Insta fails, Klein gets replaced. Russ wants to take over, so-"

"So, we're playing fine." Johanna scrolled, fingers twitching. "And Paula isn't dead. Klein is a creep."

## LIAM CLIPPERS' SLUG-STOLEN CREDIT
### IG @VCHS by @klein_truthlovepeace

"Seriously?" Paula shook her head. Her brown-blonde bob brushed the tops of her cheekbones. "Who would believe this?"

Richie tapped her stick on the gymnasium floor where the band sat side-by-side, leaning against the wall. "Georgette did."

Georgette squinted. "Huh?"

"You did?" Paula shook her head. "Seriously, Georgette?"

"Wait—huh?"

"Stop B-siding Georgette." Johanna threw her phone into her backpack. "Paula, what is going on? Did you say something to make Klein mad?"

"I don't talk to Klein."

"Well, she hates you." Richie reached over Paula's shoulder, then scrolled down on her screen. "And us. Read the caption."

Paula looked at her phone. "'McTruckney killed in car crash on October 12th... replaced by imposter singer-songwriter... Slugs have been covering up... quality of music terrible all Senior year'—well, that's not necessary, what a ho—'and Liam Clippers didn't get any credit for her songs'." She looked up. "Who's Liam Clippers?"

Richie grinned. "You're Liam Clippers."

"Huh?"

"Stop it, you're confusing Georgette." Johanna's fingers twitched. "Liam Clippers is the singer we replaced you with. After you died. Eight months ago."

"Seriously?" Paula's bob brushed her cheeks. "Klein's going to fail Journalism once teachers see these posts. She might even get suspended."

"I know." Johanna glared at her phone. "Creep."

# EVIDENCE DRIES UP THE SLUGS

IG @VCHS by @russruss66

Mrs. Gibb sucked on the end of her pen. "This doesn't look good, Paula. Or should I say—Liam."

"Very funny." Paula leaned over her teacher's desk. The rest of The Slugs stood behind her for support. "Will you tell Klein to delete these? If my parents see the posts they'll be B-sided."

"Are they still in Scotland? For your father's work?"

"Yes."

"Where they've been all year?"

"…yes."

"Since October?"

Paula glared at her teacher. "Since September. That's why they legally approved my adult status. So I could stay here for school when they moved. You were in that meeting last June. You signed the paperwork."

"Of course." Mrs. Gibb jabbed her phone screen with her pen. "But you can't blame me for asking. Klein's evidence is fairly convincing."

"Canva'd dumps from our Valentine's gig aren't convincing evidence." Johanna stepped beside Paula, fingers twitching. "Anyone can edit a photo."

"You can't blame me." Mrs. Gibb pointed her pen at The Slugs. "Your song lyrics have been fairly bleak this year-"

"That's because school has been cancelled three times since we've been Sophomores and we've been forced to stay in our bedrooms, doing class over Microsoft Teams-"

"-and your catchiest song? 'Stupid Bloody Tuesday'?" Mrs. Gibb sucked on her pen. "October 12th was a Tuesday. Were your ears always like that, Paula?"

## LAZY COVER ART OR LAZY COVER UP?
IG @VCHS by @klein_truthlovepeace

"She's insulting our album cover?" Johanna slapped the side of Georgette's bass case. "When we find that creep I'm going to kill-"

"Keep calm." Richie wedged herself between the lead singer and Georgette as The Slugs walked down the hallway on their way to the journalism room. "If a teacher hears you we'll get sent home. Paula, did you reach your dad?"

"Not yet." Paula redialed as The Slugs strode through a set of doors. "But if we get Klein to delete these, it's fine."

"It wasn't lazy cover art." Johanna swiped right. "I staged everything, but the improv'd photo looked better. AHHH!" She swung her backpack off her shoulder and kicked it, sending it flying down the hall. "It's doubleB to say Paula's dead, but way worse to post I'm a bad graphic designer. I'm going to kill her! And I don't need to make up a car accident to get away with-"

"What's wrong with our album cover?" Paula picked up Johanna's bag as The Slugs strode past the autobody garage, handing it off as she redialed. "That pic got the most shares all year."

"Creep says it's either lazy design or the image shows secret clues about your death. That the licence plate on Jo Jo's car is a code. And our outfits look like we're going to your funeral-"

"Seriously?" Paula laughed. "See, Georgette? I told you something bad would happen when you forgot to bring our costumes to the shoot."

"Huh?"

"-and look." Johanna waved her phone. "Your right hand is in front of your body, but everyone knows you're a lefty." She scratched her arm. "Lazy cover art. I'm gonna kill Klein."

## SLUGS THINK STUDENTS TOO SLIMED TO SEE
IG @VCHS by @her_ash

"Your writers' headlines are getting worse, Klein." Johanna tapped her desk with the edge of her phone. "Kind of like your sourcing."

Klein smirked. She peered across the classroom through her round, black-framed glasses and brushed her shaggy hair off her forehead. She waggled her fingers at the students sitting behind her as they frantically typed on their laptops. "I think our sourcing is great, Fab Four. We check everything twice."

"Don't call us that." Johanna leaned towards the shaggy reporter. "You lie about everything twice. It's easy to claim something's evidence when you invent too much to disprove."

"Wait." Georgette dropped her phone. "Do you think we think our class is basic? We don't. Even if we did, we wouldn't say it."

Klein chuckled. "It would be embarrassing for you to admit someone was basic—huh?"

Georgette squinted her foggy eyes. "Huh?"

"Klein, explain something." Paula crossed her arms. "You woke up this morning and thought, 'I'm going to spread lies about The Slugs and there will be zero consequences.' Are you that cheugy? Seriously?"

"They aren't lies—I'm trying to help you. I think you're great. I'm a fan of the Fab Four." Klein held up her fingers in her signature sign. "Truth plus Love equals Peace."

Richie swiped left. "'In The Slugs new single featured at Saturday's Spring Fling, 'Nowhere Woman', OG bandmates leave clues aplenty—WTF does aplenty mean?—including lyrics like, 'roll over silent woman' and 'we buried Paula', which prove that The Slugs think it's time for the truth to come out'."

Klein smirked. "See, Fab Four? I want to help. Peace."

## WHO YOU GONNA CALL? SLUG BUSTERS

IG @VCHS by @russruss66

Johanna leapt up, shaking her phone at Klein. "When did you create a school TikTok account?"

The Slugs scrambled out of their chairs and over their desks to view the new share, knocking over their backpacks in their rush.

Klein smirked. "You'd be surprised what you can accomplish when you don't waste your time writing boring music in a B-side band. Peace, Fab Four."

"You are a creep." Paula exhaled loudly as The Slugs watched the video. "So, you bought our track off Beatport just to make fun of us? Seriously? You're pathetic."

"Keep calm." Richie poked Paula's shoulder. "Watch."

Klein and the rest of the school's journalism crew frolicked around the track and field lanes in an intricate and poorly executed dance. Words scrolled along the bottom of the screen, detailing the extent of The Slug's conspiracy in musical parody.

"This is good." Georgette squinted, then smiled. "I like how you rhymed investigation with insubordination, Klein."

"It's a creepy rhyme!" Johanna threw her phone at Klein who caught it in one hand, then gently placed in on her desk. Johanna scratched her arm, angrily. "No wonder you have to hurt people—so nobody notices how untalented you are."

"Johanna-"

"This is basic!" Johanna scratched her scalp, furiously. "I was going solo this summer and now no one will care about anything I drop. They'll be too obsessed trying to figure out if Paula's dead."

"I'm not dead. Come on!" Paula laughed—then paused. "Once everyone sees me on Monday these rumours will go away. Right, Richie? Georgette? Johanna?"

## SLUG STONE OVERTURNED,
## LEAD SINGER TELLS ALL
### SOLITARY LIVERS GUILD
Episode 69: Zero Blog X with Klein Kleinster

"Thank you, Johanna, for joining me on Victoria High's podcast, Solitary Livers Guild."

"Happy to be here, Klein."

"Having you share the truth about Paula's death so quickly—the same day the conspiracy was revealed—says a lot about you as an artist. Would you say you're the best in the band, Johanna?"

"Lead singers tend to get labeled that way, but The Slugs have always been equal. We're the best when we work as a team."

"In everything?"

"When it matters."

"Like when you witnessed Paula dying in a car crash on October 12th and the three of you didn't report it and, instead, gave a makeover to your cousin, Liam Clippers, who—as my brilliant reporter, Russ Russel, found out— moved here in 2027 around the same time Paula died so she could replace the dead songwriter for The Slugs, thus allowing the band to continue its trek to local stardom and avoid the unpleasantness of you and your friends becoming unloved and obsolete?"

"Wow."

"Wow is right, Johanna. And what do you have to say about the interesting info my second brilliant reporter, Ash Asher, unearthed? That Paula wanted to leave The Slugs at the end of Junior year. That you made her stay. That you were so focused on fame you were willing to do anything to make sure The Slugs kept playing together. Anything."

"Are you accusing me of conspiracy to commit murder?"

"Are you denying it?"

## ENRAGED SLUG DESTROYS
## VCHS RECORDING ROOM
IG @VCHS by @klein_truthlovepeace

Richie tapped her stick on the cafeteria table. "That didn't go great, Johanna."

"Thanks, Rich. That is helpful feedback."

"No need for the tone, Jude."

"Stop it. I hate that nickname."

"Aren't nicknames supposed to be part of a real name? Jude has nothing to do with Johanna, so how is that a nickname?"

"Stop it, Georgette."

"Don't be mean to her, Johanna. It's not her fault you did the interview with Klein-"

"You said I should do it, Richie!"

"-and lost your temper after she accused us of murdering Paula-"

"I was trying to protect the band!"

"-and threw Asher's laptop out the window."

"Ash Asher is doubleB." Johanna scratched her ear. "High schools don't need three students in the writing program. And they shouldn't run their podcast on the fifth floor. Everyone knows recording studios are better in basements."

Squint. "The basement is where the wrestlers practice."

Johanna sighed. "Shut up, Georgette."

Paula's hair brushed her cheekbones. "This is a nightmare."

"Why doesn't anyone believe us?" Richie hucked her drumstick across the cafeteria. "Has anyone texted you, Paula? Or DM'd? Just to check if you're okay? What about Twitter?"

"Twitter? Seriously? Nope." Paula stared at her screen. The post comments kept on coming. "They all believe Klein. And Russ and Asher." She looked up. "How is this good reporting? I'm alive."

# OPD IS SAD FOR ME

IG @VCHS by @russruss66

"Klein sure is obsessed with Oakland." Georgette scrolled down. "You got that backpack button from your mom, right? Paula?"

"Yes. And it doesn't say OPD, it says OPP. Not 'Officially Pronounced Dead'. Oakland Police Department. My grandpa worked for the force in the sixties."

"See? Oakland. Oh, uh—I forgot to tell you." Georgette squinted. "When Johanna was yelling I called the phone number Klein tagged in the last caption. A guy answered and said it was the Oakland Department of Waste Security." Georgette slowly blinked her eyes. "Toilet safety is important out East, huh?"

"Stop it." Johanna picked up a rock and hurled it into the sky. It bounced down the risers, then landed on the dirt path that ran around the football field. "What are we going to do?"

"We have to carry on. Keep calm." Richie spun her drumstick between her fingers. "Everyone will get bored of Klein's lies in a few days. Everybody will find another thread to obsess over this weekend. Everything will be back to normal on Monday."

"And, again, I'm not dead. Seriously." Paula swiped left. "So."

"Did you reach your dad?" Richie's stick spun faster. "My sister's in a What'sApp groupchat with him, if you want her to-"

"Keeps going to voicemail." Paula swiped right. "It's fine. We always talk on Saturday, so it'll be fine. He doesn't have an Insta account anyway—and my mom still follows that I-Hate-Technology influencer. It's fine."

"Uh, Paula?" Georgette held out her phone. "Sorry. My mom just texted me. I told her about Klein's posts and she shared them with her Meta group and your dad saw them and he spun to the B-side." Squint. "My bad."

## LIES PROTECT SLUGS, FAMILY UNDER THE SLIME
### IG @VCHS by @klein_truthlovepeace

"-and then Lizzy emailed me a link so I could join Mr. Rigby's group-"

"Dad."

"-and I saw what that awful reporter was saying about you-"

"Dad."

"-and all my friends were commenting on the posts. Carol said, 'good riddance' and Sadie said she wants to start a GoFundMe campaign to raise money for that poor Liam Clippers."

"Your friends are B-side, Dad. Liam Clippers isn't a person."

"She is a person, I googled her. But then I got your messages and, seriously—Paula—I don't know what to believe."

"Dad…"

"There is an obituary for you online. An obituary! I saw it! Lucille emailed me the link. You have no idea how awful this has been for me, stuck here in the UK with your mother who-"

"Dad!" Paula breathed as her father snivelled. "Dad, these are lies. We'll talk over Zoom tomorrow. You'll see."

"What if you're a video hoax? Maggie Mae told me about those. Criminals use greenscreens and face filters-"

"Dad. I am alive. You can ask me questions when we talk on Saturday. Tomorrow. Okay?"

"But Pam told me that our phones are always recording our conversations for the ad men. You know I'm a verbal processor. What if when I'm coming up with questions to ask you my phone sends my voice to the ad men and they sell it to the criminals and that awful reporter creates a video where fake you has all the answers-"

"Dad."

## STUDENTS CONFIRM PROOF, RUMOURS TRUE
IG @VCHS by @klein_truthlovepeace

On Monday morning, Paula strode through the school's courtyard as it rapidly filled with the rest of her class. She ignored the stares of her classmates. The rest of the band followed close behind.

Whispers followed close behind.

*"I heard The Slugs stole our January ELA diploma to make their secret messages. You know—that quote from King Lear?"*

*"Russ told me that the lyrics in 'I Am the Sea Cow' prove that Paula—I mean, Liam—is definitely an imposter."*

*"Mrs. Gibb showed me a poem that proves Paula is dead. Some ancient named Joyce James predicted this would happen a hundred years ago and now it has."*

Paula broke away from the band and strode towards the fountain that stood in the middle of the courtyard.

*"I heard that Paula used to like chicken before she went vegetarian which is why Liam wrote about Humpty Dumpty in 'Suzy in the Clouds with Emeralds'. Liam wants the truth to come out, too. She thinks the coverup is B-side."*

Paula swung her backpack off her shoulder as she reached the fountain. Klein walked out of the school flipping the Peace sign, her journalism crew tight at her heels.

*"Ash told me The Slugs have been fighting for months and Johanna told her the truth so they could finally break up."*

Paula removed a bucket from her backpack. She held the bucket under the water that cascaded from the fountain's spout. She stared at the waterfall as her bucket filled. A smile pricked at the corners of her mouth.

Klein walked closer, fingers raised. "I see the Fab Four is showing a united front today. Think that'll be enough to keep suppressing the facts?"

*"Mrs. Gibb said that Klein's getting a special scholarship at the end of the year. Uncovering a scandal like this one means success for life! Klein is so gifted. I wish I could be as smart as-"*

Paula swung around and doused the shaggy reporter with the bucket of water. The students in the courtyard gasped. They stared at the soaked journalist as she spun to face Paula, shrieking. The students raised their phones, eager to see what Klein would do next and ready to record the action that would fuel the gossip that filled their feeds.

Klein sputtered, spitting water from her mouth as she whipped her dripping glasses from her face. "Look, Paula—you're dead!"

Paula smiled. The bucket slipped from her fingers, falling to the courtyard cobblestones with a *clang!* She brushed her brown-blonde hair out of her eyes and smirked at the waterlogged reporter. "Oh. I don't agree with that."

# BALLOON BELOVED

## 7

I curl my fingers around the edge of the basket. The air currents buffet against the side of the balloon, tipping me and Laurel as we struggle to keep our footing. Laurel presses her back into the corner of the basket and crouches down, out of the wind. I lean over the edge, peering up at the sky. The sun hits my face, warming my cheeks as I gaze at the other Hot Airs that fill our surrounding airspace, lifting and descending as the air cools then warms around them. We drift through a cloud. I stick out my hand, running my fingers through its wet mist. The cloud is cold. Beads of water drip from my fingers, falling into the ocean miles below.

"Don't lean out too far." Laurel clings to her safety tethers as she crouches in her corner. Releasing the nylon straps, she adjusts our weighted ballasts and the balloon basket stabilizes. Laurel exhales—then relaxes. She starts braiding her hair, tucking her plaits into her Nomex jacket after she finishes.

I shake my dripping fingers. "You worry too much."

"You don't worry enough."

I lean farther out, stretching my hand up into the atmosphere.

"Jean. Stop it."

I glance back at Laurel. She's scowling in her corner. I pull my hand back inside the basket. "Today might be the day."

"You say that every morning."

"Because every morning might be the day."

Laurel re-braids her pigtail. "Just—don't lean out too far."


"Laurel! Laurel, look!" I kneel beside my friend and shake her arm. She wakes, grunting, then blinks up at me. I shake her harder. "There's a new one. I told you today was the day."

I scramble to my feet and tip to the basket's edge. Clutching the woven wicker I point my finger into the sky, towards the nearest balloon. Its envelope is brightly-coated, new seeming. The girl pulling on its flying wires wears a flight suit that matches the nylon parachute—pink and yellow, with red vertical stripes running up its seams. She is perfect.

"Hallooo!" I raise my voice so the girl can hear me over the puffing vents. She turns, her loose hair blowing in the wind, and a smile splits her face. She raises her hand and calls back—but I can't hear her.

"Laurel, help me get closer." I yank on the steering cables and turn the gauge on the helium tank to max. Our balloon jolts upwards and Laurel shrieks. I laugh, watching her tumble to the back of our basket.

She clutches her tethers. "Jean, I swear on the sky, if you tip us-"

"Help me get closer."

The girl's balloon changes direction, bumping through the mass of neighbouring Hot Airs.

"Stop trying to steer." Laurel grips our aluminum cable and swings her agile body over to me. "You have to give this up. You're never going to reach her. You're dense."

"No." I shake my head, squinting through the sun as the perfect girl's balloon floats away. "Today's the day."

I hold a wing over our Hot Air's burner, roasting our lunch hour catch—a seagull. Licking juices off my chin, I glare at Laurel. "You should have helped me."

"Just give up." Laurel sucks on the seagull's beak. "The basketmate policy isn't so bad. The Submersion made it impossible to find love and having assigned mates is nice. Accept it, Jean. Everyone else has."

I stare at the wing, watching it slowly char. I thrust the burnt meat at Laurel before she makes me so mad I throw the thing over the edge. She takes the hot wing and blows on it, then gingerly picks at the meat with her sooty fingers. Our balloon rises and falls gently in the morning currents, swaying beside the others. I stand, wipe my greasy hands on my flight pants, then look over the edge of our basket, hoping to see my girl again. But the pink and yellow balloon is gone. Its red vertical stripes have disappeared.

"No." I look down at Laurel—she's picking at the seagull's foot. "I finally saw her, so we have to get her back. I believe in true love and I believe she's the one. Please. Help me?"

Laurel spits a gull claw out of her mouth, over her shoulder. It soars over the edge of the basket and falls through the sky.

I watch the claw spiral towards the ocean as long as I can before it becomes invisible. We're high up that day. It's chilly. The sun cuts through the clouds and turns the water green, instead of the sludgy brown I've known my whole life. "Please, Laurel? You're supposed to be my friend."

"I'm not your friend, I'm your mate." Laurel licks her fingers. "But I care about you, so—fine."

I scramble to her side. "Really?"

"This one time. Then, when this doesn't work out, you'll accept that out-of-basket love is impossible and move on."

"One time is all I need. It is possible." I stretch my hand, brushing a wisp with my fingers. Water collects on my palm. "You'll see."


Laurel pulls on the steering cables. Our balloon floats through the air, navigating around a cluster of neighbours. I lean over the edge of the basket, peering through the envelopes that crowd the sky, looking for my girl's vertical red stripes. Laurel grunts and our balloon slips between two old-fashioned Hoppers. How they've survived the last fifty years, I have no idea. And I don't care.

Laurel is helping me find my girl.

The sun is nearing its zenith when I see the stripes. "Laurel! Hold!"

"Are you joking? I can barely steer this thing in the direction you want. I can't stop."

"Then slow down! Slower!"

We're nearing my beloved's balloon. I can see her, perfect and smiling. She's indistinct—being so far away and partially blocked by cables, her basket and the decorative tassels that hang from the edges of her envelope—but I can see her. My beloved.

Our balloon swings abruptly, caught in a stronger air current. Laurel whirls around, scowling. "Jean, lean back. You're such a-"

Swears stream out of Laurel's mouth, louder than our puffing helium canister. I grip the edge of the basket and twist as our balloon rights itself, but I never take my gaze off my beloved's balloon. Pink and yellow and red.

"You camel." Laurel grunts. "You're too reckless. One day-"

I raise my hand, cutting off her cruel monologue. "You know why I hate you? Because you talk like that. You've forced me to look for true love elsewhere."

"Don't blame me for your narcissistic idealism, you porcupine."

"Can you get us closer? If you get our basket next to hers I can climb over."

"You can what?"

"Climb into my beloved's basket."

"You can't do that! That would violate the constitution! And what I am supposed to do, live here by myself? And what about her basketmate? You think they want a threesome? It'd never work, there'd be too much weight, you'll die and-"

"You think too much." The perfect girl nears. I can see her smile. "Just get me closer and we'll figure out the rest."


A stiff wind keeps my beloved's balloon out of reach, hovering within the clouds, smushed inside a cluster of

Montgolfiers. I moan, then hit the edge of our basket with the heel of my hand. "Laurel! Look what you did."

Her seagull beak hits the side of my face. I wipe my cheek and wrench my eyes away from the vertical stripes to glare at my basketmate.

Laurel scowls back. "If you keep being mean to me I'm not going to help you."

"Just get us back to her." I turn to my beloved and watch as her balloon breaks free, rising up and out of the cluster. "Today's the day."

We hunt my beloved's balloon the entire afternoon. Laurel steers us past clouds and birds, Hot Airs and drones, repair-lanterns and artillery-floaters. She is diligent and doesn't give up, and as the hours pass we draw closer and closer to the pink and yellow Roziere. My beloved is in the Air Force; the nearer we get the clearer the Orbiter symbol emblazoned on the side of her basket becomes. She is fierce. She has to be to belong to the Elite Flyers. My beloved is perfect.

We draw closer. Laurel starts to sweat, soaking through her flight suit. Her musk fills my mind, distracting me from my target. "Can you move upwind?"

"Do you want my help or not?"

"It's just-" I purse my lips, not wanting to make Laurel angrier. "Hurry up."

Three Diversion Balloons block our path.

"Laurel!"

"Jean?"

"Don't hit them!"

"I'm not going to hit them."

"You're getting too close. We're going to lose my beloved."

"We can make it through. Be buoyant."

"No, they're too big. Dense Diversions."

"They're good ones, though. When was the last time you saw a Minion?"

"I don't care, just get us by."

We float between the story-inspired Hot Airs.

Laurel grunts. "See? I didn't hit them."

I clutch the edge of our basket. "You almost lost my beloved."

We float closer to the red stripes.

Laurel winds the steering cable around our basket knob. "I need a break."

I whip around, furious. "We're almost there. Almost there!"

"We're in the crosscurrent of the horse latitude and the westerly. They'll carry us to her. Be patient." Laurel squats down and rifles through her sack. She removes a black beaten-up object and hucks it at me—her binoculars. "Use those. Make sure your true love is worth all this."

I raise the dented eyepiece to my face and aim it towards my beloved. Her smiling smile fills the viewfinder. I laugh. "Oh, she is worth it."

"What about her mate?"

I shift the binoculars to the side. A scruffy head fills the viewfinder. I laugh again. "Nothing to worry about. My beloved will choose me over them, for sure."

"Jean?"

I lower the binoculars. Laurel bites her lip, a habit I hate. The repair-lanterns rarely drop us personal supplies like balm and Laurel's cracked lips make me nauseous. Swallowing the surge of bile that pushes at the back of my throat I clench my teeth, then smile at my sunburnt mate. "What?"

"What's the plan?"

I raise the binocular's eyepiece again. My beloved's face is all I can see. "We reach her balloon and make a switch: me for her basketmate. I get to be happy, finally, and you won't be alone." I lower the eyepiece and look down at my sweaty mate. "That's what you want, isn't it?"

Lighting streaks across the darkened sky.

Just as our balloon moved close enough to my beloved's to make the switch, the sun set and the night delayed my dream from coming true. Then the storm came, thundering around us as the wind howled and the rain beat against our faces.

But I was determined. I kept Laurel focused on my goal. "Hurry up."

"Jean, we have to turn back."

"What?"

"The storm! It's too big. We have to ride the currents out of here."

"I can't hear you."

"We're going to get struck."

"Just keep going."

"If lightning hits us it'll take days before the lanterns send supplies—if we're buoyant and land on the water face up. I don't want to drown over some girl you've never met and-"

"We're so close."

"Jean!"

Lightning strikes our envelope, exploding the helium canister in a burst of fire and smoke. The downpour drenches the burning tank and puts out the danger of our envelope catching fire—but the worst has happened. We tumble out of the sky, towards the sea, hurtling through the atmosphere like the comet that triggered the Submersion. I hear Laurel screaming, a high-pitched whine that rips out of her mouth and is swallowed by the storm. I clutch the edge of the basket, thanking the tethers for their high-quality manufacturing even while I curse my luck: Laurel has failed and my dream is lost. I've lost my beloved.

We bob in the ocean. Laurel flips open the seal of her water bottle, then pours a stream of rainwater into her cracked mouth. The mouth I'll be stuck with until I die.

Laurel tosses the bottle in my direction. "You have to drink."

I don't catch it. I let the bottle fall, then watch it roll around the base of the basket, shifting as the gentle waves rock us. The sun bakes the back of my neck, making me parched, but I refuse to budge. "Leave me alone."

"We'll be back in the air soon. Drink."

"I hate you."

Laurel re-braids her hair. "You are such a peacock. Once the lanterns drop the supplies I'll patch the hole and refill the tank."

"She's gone."

"Yup."

"I'll never find her again."

"Probably not."

I kick the bottle at Laurel. It bounces off her shin. She smirks and takes another pull of water. I drop my head, resting it on the edge of the basket. It's too heavy to hold up. "How could you do this to me?"

"I told you—you're dense. Switching balloons is impossible. It's never been done."

"You could have tried harder."

A gauzy orange repair-lantern appears in the cloudless sky, beeping as it floats into our basket. The delivery drone skitters out of the lantern on its spindly legs and drops a vinyl-wrapped package in Laurel's lap. She grins, then unwraps the slippery fabric as the delivery drone skitters back into the lantern and the gauzy orange flyer rises into the air. Laurel crawls over to our nylon envelope, which she'd folded into a neat square after we'd crashed. She crouches over the tear. I watch her fix the hole—her tongue sticks out between her cracked lips as she works and her sooty face screws up as she concentrates.

I squeeze my eyes shut. "You could have tried harder."

Our balloon floats gently in the crosscurrents. The brisk wind raises the hair on my arms and I clutch the edge of the basket until my knuckles turn white. I peer through the crowd of balloons in our airspace, searching.

"Anything?" Laurel tips over to my side, peering into the sky with me.

"Of course not. You lost my only chance at happiness."

"Don't be a giraffe."

"Don't be dense!"

Our basket sways in the wind. The nylon envelope carries us where it pleases. We drift past clouds and birds, Hot Airs and drones, repair-lanterns and artillery-floaters. A cluster of Diversions shaped like Obi Wan and a bun-headed woman float by. But there's no pink and yellow, red vertically-striped Roziere.

My beloved is gone.

"Jean?" Laurel puts her hand on my arm. I shake it off. She grunts. "You know, Jean—you might have another chance at happiness."

"No."

"You might."

"I won't."

"She's not the only girl in the sky."

"She's the only perfect girl in the sky."

"Maybe." Laurel tugs on her braids. "Maybe not."

I whirl around, then unleash the emotion I've been holding in my chest. I hurl my anger at Laurel like the meteor that ripped through the stratosphere. "Finding the perfect girl was impossible, but I did it. You said, 'You're dense,' but I wasn't. No one has ever caught their one true love, not since the Submersion—except for me. I found her. I knew I would, some day. Now she's gone." I stare at my basketmate, who's gazing through the clouds. I stare at her sweaty, sooty, sunburnt face—and sigh. "You won't help me again, will you?"

"What did I say?"

I stare into the clouds. "Didn't think so."

"But you might still be happy."

I laugh. "How?"

Laurel lets go of the edge of the basket and tips away, crouching in her corner. She pulls out her left plait and re-braids her hair. She smiles at me, then tucks her pigtail into her Nomex jacket. The wind disappears and our Hot Air hovers between two clouds, unmoving.

Static. Still.

Silent.

The dry heat electrifies the hair on the back of my neck as Laurel's eyes lock on my face and her lids slowly narrow. She licks her cracked lips, then her smiling smile widens. "Just—don't lean out too far."

# DO NOT TALK TO THAT CHILD

# 8

*Monday, March 21, 2044*
Super 8, North Richmond
ENTRY #40

It's the beginning of another week—my last here in Victoria. After spending the weekend going through my notes I'm happy to report that the evidence I gathered in support of DNTTTC's initiative has been overwhelmingly positive. The children in this city are mature, well-adjusted and show signs of healthy developmental growth over the past decade. I have one family left to interview, but I'm certain their story will coincide with the others.

*Reporting from previous week:*
**Family 26 Stats** two guardians/fraternal twins—age 9
-siblings have never met—both believe they are OC*

-parents have effectively supported sibling's separated lives (coordinated virtual work schedules to maintain illusion of independence, created rotating routines to include adult interaction, support the security bots that protect their children's individual spaces)

-each child maintains a 3.87 GPA in their courses, demonstrates high-functioning organization, cleanliness and emotional self-regulation, and are in peak physical condition

-twins were born after CSM** was passed in province—neither indicates an awareness of AC***

-parents show signs of stress (mother divulged she wished divorce could be option for them), but both are committed to CSM and will remain together to protect their offspring until the twin's minority status expires

*Only Child
**Child-Separation Mandate
***Additional Children


**Family 27 Stats** two guardians/two children—age 14, 17

-siblings have not interacted in ten years—both believe they are OC

-parents keep them separate, though father has mobility issues which has increased the difficulty in maintaining the illusion, but mother has sizeable Trust income and is able to afford full-time care for spouse, including apartment management services

-each child maintains < 3.0 GPA in their courses, demonstrates above-average organization, cleanliness and emotional self-regulation (for post-pubescent youth), and are in exemplary physical condition (private trainer comes by twice a day to facilitate fitness program on rooftop coordinated with other families in complex)

-neither have any memory of when they lived together (and were exposed to AC)

-parents show no signs of stress; both feel supported by DNTTTC and are excited for the upcoming year when 17's minority status expires

**Family 28 Stats** guardian/dependant/children—age 6, 8, 11
-6, 8 have never met AC; 11 has not interacted with AC in ten years—6 revealed she hears things through the apartment's walls (does not know what she hears, believes it's an avatar or other media source)—11 claims to have vague memories of AC prior to CSM, but cannot articulately describe these memories

-parent keeps siblings separate with occasional assistance from senior dependant (parent's mother)—senior dependant admits she struggles with CSM, but respects her son's wishes to protect his offspring

-each child sits between 1.8-2.9 GPA in their courses, demonstrates below-average* organization, cleanliness and emotional self-regulation skills (could be due to the fact there is one bathroom in the household, small individual spaces and no support staff to maintain basic facilities)

-parent shows no sign of stress—he has faith in CSM and believes his offspring to be content

-dependant was hesitant to discuss her opinion of the LEG** targets, but became more transparent after I showed her my research credentials and explained the importance of this report

*still above national average
**Life/Education Growth

I'm looking forward to completing this investigation.

I'll admit, when I was first assigned the task of reporting on the unconventional practises in this city I was convinced they would be a total failure; but after several weeks, and a unified front of community-wide enthusiasm, I plan to happily advocate for DNTTTC's methodologies and recommend they be implemented across the country—immediately. Separating children from each other at birth seems to have eliminated all inner-city violence, forms of abuse and intolerance, and led to the creation of mature and evolved humans who will become effective contributors in society. Surprisingly, Mrs. Pahnk's philosophy that 'children destroy children' has been thoroughly proven. As crude as her phrasing was—"get them while they are young"—Mrs. Pahnk's diligent methodologies took into account every possible factor for efficient implementation of her CSM. Life in Victoria is flawless. From online education to adult exposure only, DNTTTC's initiative is exemplary. I am honoured to be part of the beginning phase of this new societal order.

Tomorrow I interview the final family. I'm certain the results will be consistent.


*Tuesday, March 22, 2044*
Avenue Living Community (ALC), Victoria
ENTRY #41

Met with the final family today. They were different.

*Reporting from morning:*

**Family 29 Stats:** guardian/one child /age 12

-child occupies entire apartment, not just her individual space (no need for isolation, no AC in home)—12 has never met AC but seems to be aware there are others (nothing was said explicitly, but questions were asked)

-parent lives inclusively with child at all times—they engage in all activity together, excepting when parent goes outdoors (child accepts all food, home maintenance and media deliveries, and child interacts with a multitude of adults on a regular basis—parent's childless peers)

-child speaks without first being asked, manages own educational decision making and indicates an unprecedented level of independence

-child has 4.1 GPA; demonstrates more maturity and self-regulation skills than average adult; consistently high level of competence on MPSA*

-parent shows signs of extreme distress**—nervousness, sleeplessness, rapid speech, passive body posture

-parent explicit about how they and their child follow CSM, though they did not vocally express their support for the initiative like the other parents—parent seemed frustrated by DNTTTC (I noted undercurrents of anger) which is surprising given how advanced their offspring is

*Maslow's Pyramid of Self-Actualization

**I cannot understand Guardian 29's behaviour at this time, but it might have something to do with being eclipsed by their child

I'm visiting this family again on Thursday.

I'm disturbed by the parent's obvious contempt for DNTTTC, seeing how marvellously their child is performing. Perhaps Guardian 29's constant exposure to avatars, alter egos and digital exclusivity practises has taken its toll, as we've seen in other parts of the country where DNTTTC's methods have already been adopted—though that couldn't be the case with Family 29, as the parent seemed comfortable with the meta integration in their home.

Perhaps the home itself is impacting their wellness; the apartment complexes in this city are fairly dreary, all grey brick and brownstone, and the CSM security bots operate day and night—though every family lives in the same type of dwelling and none of them exhibited this parent's level of pessimism.

It could be the weather, since autumn has been unusually rainy and, in a prairie region like this one, climate changes can impact emotional stability—though the child seemed fine. More solemn than other children, but fine.

I'm willing to attribute the parent's condition to their own exposure to AC growing up. No doubt, as Mrs. Pahnk says, there is adolescent trauma that impacts this person's ability to thrive in modern society. I will apply this psychological lens to my questioning on Thursday and see if I can find satisfactory answers.

*Wednesday, March 23, 2044*
ALC, Victoria
ENTRY #42


In order to be thorough I re-visited the families I met this past week to see if the seasonal shift affected multiple people, not just Family 29. I noted that some of the verbiage used in their initial reporting changed, tilting slightly more to the negative. The adults seemed more inclined to extrapolate on the downsides of keeping their offspring away from AC, though when I re-interviewed the children in their individual spaces their mentality remained unchanged—they still believed they were an OC and that it was dangerous to leave their homes until their minority status expired. Strange. Perhaps it *is* the weather. This is the ninth straight day of downpour, which makes robust mental health difficult to maintain. Even I am not immune to its effects.

No. It must be Guardian 29. I believe I've been unfairly influenced by the pessimistic persona of that parent. Doubts about DNTTTC have started to permeate my reflections; odd, questioning thoughts about the CSM. When I re-interview Family 29 tomorrow I will confirm my suspicions: that Guardian 29 is defunct, not the DNTTTC initiative.

*Thursday, March 24, 2044*
Super 8, North Richmond // ALC, Victoria
ENTRY #43

Prior to leaving my hotel today, I received a visit from Mrs. Pahnk. I assured her of my rave review for her CSM and promised to have my final assessment ready by tomorrow. My employer is eager to hear her story and ready for publication within the month. Mrs. Pahnk was pleased, especially when I told her she would be this province's public representative for DNTTTC—appropriate, given she is Head of the Fairfield School Wellness Association. I did admit to Mrs. Pahnk my reservations regarding Family 29. She shared the name of the parent—Mx. Murrow—and the child: Irwin. Apparently, Mx. Murrow was vocally against the initiative a decade ago, but quieted down after the death of their spouse in 2035. Mrs. Pahnk wasn't surprised to hear of Mx. Murrow's attitude and agreed that a second visit was necessary, given the circumstances.

Mrs. Pahnk is a pleasant woman. A bit eccentric, with her clipped way of speaking, slightly obsessive need for neatness and strange affection for the umbrella she always carries, but geniuses can be unconventional, so I try not to judge. I'll practice that non-judgemental attitude during my second interview with the Murrows. I'm leaving for it now. It's still raining, but Mrs. Pahnk lent me her umbrella. It's wide-brimmed with a particularly sharp tip: more than adequate. I can see why she likes it.

*//*

I just left the Murrow residence. Rather than feeling satisfied with the outcome I'm more confused. Today, Mx. Murrow wasn't anxious or upset, but rather grounded and clear-headed. They spoke succinctly about the struggles Irwin faces—from a developmental angle—and clearly articulated their concerns. I'll admit, they were convincing. I had no idea of Irwin's challenges since she presents so well around adults. The child experiences phases of muted energy, then hyper-focused intensity, accompanied by a distinctly negative perspective. I see Mx. Murrow's point about how healthy an exploration of childhood desires can be when socialization is regulated, yet unrestricted. They advocated that children should spend time together, with moderate discipline based on clearly communicated consequences for inappropriate actions, rather than simply their removal from the source of dysfunction. They claim that children need to be exposed to AC and need to connect with their uninhibited selves in order to mature in a natural way.

They used the word natural several times. The implication being that Mrs. Pahnk's initiative was unnatural.

They claimed that AC aren't the problem in society, rather that issues stem from adults behaving childishly. They said that many adults never acknowledge their inner immaturity and, instead, allow their insecurities to grow unchecked. They believe that adults don't compassionately address of their sources of strife and that leads to 18+ incidents of violence, crime, abuse and disregulation.

Most disturbingly, Mx. Murrow painted a vivid picture of a future in which our unnatural children will mature, be set free into the "wild" and regress, falling into unacknowledged habits of the aforementioned childish behaviours which will lead to an increase in brutality and dysfunction. The opposite of Pahnk's vision.

I spoke with the child some more. Irwin. I can see that she's an odd girl, even knowing her exceptional performance accomplishments. She watches everything with a deep intensity, giving one the impression she sees information others can't. Things below the surface.

But I like her. She's thoughtful and speaks with a reflective intelligence that belies her years. Though I did see flashes of childishness in her. Mx. Murrow had cake delivered to the apartment—they were celebrating some annual event (they didn't say what it was). When Irwin saw the dessert her face completely changed. She looked like a cartoon character, large-eyed and drooling—and she giggled. Giggled!

It's been a long time since I heard someone giggle.

Irwin and Mx. Murrow shared the cake, and Irwin offered me a slice. I declined—I was on the job—but there was something so sincere about Irwin's offer I almost accepted. Sincerity is a quality many adults lose as life wears them down. While I watched the Murrows eat their cake I started thinking about other childish behaviours—childlike qualities—that we lose as we age. Innocence and hope. Courage.

Trust.

I'm planning to do my own research this evening. My employer has several educators on the company payroll, so perhaps alternate, mastery level voices will shed some light on Mx. Murrow's ideology.

It's doubtful, though. The world has lived in chaos for four decades and Mrs. Pahnk's initiative offers a concrete, step-by-step solution that promises change. Mx. Murrow's ideas are vague and ill-defined. I cannot see them holding any merit.

*Friday, March 25, 2044*
ALC, Victoria // Super 8, North Richmond
ENTRY #44

I met with Irwin again today. What a remarkable child. She didn't talk much—she's very quiet—but before I left she said something interesting. She said, "I feel lonely, and I don't know why." I can't imagine what it must be like to be the only one of your kind—a child in a word of adults. I wonder if the other children in Families 1 through 28 secretly feel the same.

I spoke with my education resources yesterday. Mx. Murrow is correct. Not only did my resources confirm their opinions, they provided me with new information about childhood development that Mrs. Pahnk withheld; like that children are taught cruelty, not born knowing it, and that the human brain develops well into adults' twenties and thirties—people don't reach maturity at eighteen. I can't believe I'm saying this, but the last several weeks of my work are now tainted. Seeing everything through this new lens, where childhood isolation is harmful and the sociological implications disastrous, I've decided to change my recommendation—the entire tone of my report. My employer supports the adaptation. Apparently, she was skeptical of DNTTTC as well. I will break the news to Mrs. Pahnk later today. She's scheduled to come by to review my final assessment. And take back her umbrella.

//

Mrs. Pahnk took the news well. She understood my change of heart though was disappointed, understandably. But she respects scientific integrity and said that DNTTTC would whole-heartedly support whatever assessment my employer approved for publishing. She's a kind human, despite her eccentricities.

It really is a shame her initiative didn't work out. A decade of dedication to a project is a sizeable investment— with an entire city committed to the work—but I don't see how DNTTTC could ever possibly be effective, big picture.

Children need to be children. They need to run and jump, climb and fall, break their bones and break their hearts. They need to hurt and recover, over and over, with loving, consistent adults by their side. They need unconditional freedom to make mistakes—and accountability to learn from them—and feel safe to live in their world: their strange, subculture world that exists for such a brief period of time.

When I was twelve, I remember being at a party. My friends were there. Not my extracurricular friends, my academic friends. We were playing some board game. Trivial Pursuit, I think, and it was my turn to answer a question.

I knew a lot about life when I was a teen. I'd been exposed to maltreatment and I had this thirst to understand the world. Perhaps to know why in such a beautiful place with such beautiful possibility people allowed cruelty to go unaddressed. So, I studied feverishly in school. I was motivated to learn as much as I could. I felt as though I was driven to find the answers—to what, I didn't know, but I was studious and I tried, really hard.

I knew a lot of information when I was a teenager, but I didn't know the answer to the question on my Trivial Pursuit card.

My friends laughed at me when I got it wrong. They called me names, said that for an advanced placement student I was really slow. They pitied me, patted my shoulder, rolled their eyes and shook their heads. They whispered behind my back—whispered words of unkindness, of judgement. The worst one leaned over and hissed in my ear, "It's okay. Not everyone gets to be smart. You're nice and that's important."

I was mortified. I wanted to cry, but was loath to give them the satisfaction of seeing me in pain. I went home that night and opened my family desktop, sliding the Encarta 95 disc into the CD-rom, searching for the answer to the question, *What is the capital of Taiwan.*

Taipei. The answer was Taipei.

When I was a child, AC often made me feel like I wasn't good enough. They often hurt me deeply. But, for all their faults—the embarrassments, betrayals, outbursts—I wouldn't trade that time for anything. I was challenged by AC. Tested by AC. I laughed with additional children.

We laughed at everything. We laughed at the wind blowing our skirts around our ankles. Laughed at the melting popsicles that dribbled down our chins. Laughed at the chalk pictures we drew on sidewalks, mosquito bites acquired on camping trips, ghost stories told at all-night sleepovers. First kisses, first stirrings, first lies. Failing grades, public shame, donuts in the ice-covered high school parking lot. Laughed at failed attempts at liquid liner and cried as it ran down our cheeks when *he* dated someone else.

We loved when we were children. We loved deeply, and it hurt. We loved best friends and closest family, comforting teachers and uplifting mentors—frantically, and with no thought at all about the risk involved. We loved ourselves and all our flaws, and we loved with the sweet sorrow of longing to be someone better, longing for the day we'd figure it all out. Longing to know everything, become an adult and leave our messy, name-calling, laughter-ridden, love-filled, absolutely thrilling childhood in the past. And it was left in the past, pushed away, forced into memory and forgotten. I forgot my childhood.

Until a girl named Irwin giggled and it all came rushing back.

I'm flying home tomorrow. I'll be sad to leave this little town. It's been my home for many weeks and I've become fond of it. It rained less today. The forecast says the sun will shine for my trip back to Oakland. I'll check in with the Murrows before I go, to assure them DNTTTC will be shut down after my piece goes national. Mx. Murrow will be so relieved, I know it. They'll tell the other parents. Irwin—and other separated children—will now have the chance to reclaim the life they lost. The healing can begin. I know that's what this city actually wants: to be able to recapture that thrill of childhood.

Mar. 26/44

DNTTTC

School Wellness Association, FAIRFIELD

RECORD 1A

Day one.

*The Globe* editor accepted offer to write article about Do Not Talk To That Child's Child Separation Mandate. She was sympathetic to cause after explanation that specialist from Oakland University disappeared. Starting study from beginning. Will include every detail. Glad to be international rep for my work.

Reported to regional police first incident of violence in city this decade: twins from Twenty-sixth family unit stole Child Twenty-nine from apartment and killed her in the street. I insisted regional police not punish twins for their crime: they are young—ruthless and bloodthirsty—and once maturity is reached these behaviours will be gone. Regional police understand my program will make the world a better place.

Guardian Twenty-nine is upset. Moving out of province. They will preach of effectiveness of Do Not Talk To That Child. Glad to see my good word spread.

Meeting with First family unit this afternoon. Will record their satisfaction following School Wellness Association's Child Accountability Rubric, an educator-generated reference material backed by Prime Minister Patricia. Glad to have national support to ensure Do Not Talk To That Child's success.

Must clean umbrella. Oakland University Specialist and Child Twenty-nine made it messy.

Planning to write addendum outlining trauma in adults triggered by Additional Children. *Globe* editor promised to publish as novel. Book contract in development. Glad to have the opportunity to fully share about the horrors of childhood.

# FIXING IT

# 9

Grasshoppers chirped within the wheat fields. The alien ship landed on the lawn that stretched out in front of the farmhouse. Old Denny rocked on her porch chair as she watched the extraterrestrial climb out of its spacecraft. Old Denny turned, then yelled over her shoulder, "Kim! Your turn!"

A grubby girl with dirt on her nose stuck her head out the farmhouse door. "Now?"

"Yes, girl. Grab your sack."

Kimberly sighed loudly, throwing her hands in the air. She disappeared into the farmhouse, then clomped out onto the porch holding a bag in her hands. "Where is he?"

"By the wheat field."

"Jesus Mary, I have a test tomorrow."

"This is more important than some school test. Get."

"Dang it, Denny." Kimberly clomped down the porch steps and across the lawn.

Old Denny rocked as she watched Kimberly follow the extraterrestrial into its craft. The door closed behind them and the ship flew into the sky. Dusk descended, turning the sky violet streaked with blue—darker than it usually became. The blinking lights that covered the circular spaceship seemed to deepen the inky celestial blackness that wrapped around the farm.

Old Denny spit. "Good timing. That girl needs to Fix-It, real bad."

The sun rose. The grasshoppers stirred, flipping their wings to free them from morning dew. Old Denny sat at the kitchen table, smoking. Kimberly gnawed on her apple as she reviewed her notes for the day's exam.

Old Denny took a drag on her cigarette. "Well?"

"Well, what?"

"You gonna tell your gran who it was?"

Kimberly sighed, letting her half-eaten apple drop onto her notebook. "Sure. It was little me. When I was five."

Old Denny grinned around her smoke. "Thought so."

"You did?"

"Uh huh. We all knew about your Evil."

"All of you?"

"Your mam, your granpa, your sis. We knew about it when it happened."

Kimberly stared at her fruit. "Wish I didn't know about it."

"We all have to face our Evil, some day. Best if you find out about it when you're still young. Gives you lots of time to Fix-It." Old Denny fiddled with her cigarette. "Know what you're gonna do?"

"Not yet."

"Revenge?"

"Nah."

Old Denny nodded. "Good girl. I never like it when folk take that route. Give your Evil-Maker a talkin' to, then?"

"I don't want to."

"Nobody does." Old Denny tapped Kimberly's apple with the end of her cigarette. Ash fell onto the notebook. "Listen to me, girl. The quicker you do it, the better. You have the backing of the whole town. We've been waiting for this day so we can get that bastard out. We all hate 'im, after what he did to you. But you have to start it. Then we can follow and run him out of here."

Kimberly closed her eyes. She rubbed her temples. "It's so embarrassing."

"For him."

Kimberly stilled, then smiled at her grandmother. "Thanks, Denny."


Grasshoppers chirped on the balcony. Ava stuck her head into her children's bedroom, watching as her husband tucked the boys under their coverlets. "Sugar? The ship's here."

Lucas straightened. "Tonight? Where?"

"In the foyer."

"Inside the building?" Lucas jogged out of the boys' room, then grabbed his coat from the front closet. "I didn't think they came inside."

"No, sorry. They're beside the foyer. On the street."

Lucas swore as he struggled into his jacket. "I'm going to get a ticket. How long have they been there?"

"Two minutes?"

"That's not too bad." Lucas kissed his wife. "See you in the morning." He jogged out the door and into his condo's hallway.

Ava called after him as he neared the stairwell that wound down to the lobby. "Will you be eighteen?"

Lucas paused. His hand gripped the stairwell door's handle. "Hope so."

The sun rose. The grasshoppers lay on the balcony, barely moving after the hard overnight frost. Ava blew on her cup of coffee as Lucas stumbled out of their bedroom, half asleep. He sank down on the couch and she handed him a second cup. "Here, sweets. It's fresh."

"Thanks."

"Milk and sugar, sugar?"

"Black's fine." He took a deep drink. "Good beans, love."

"Thanks, sweets."

"Do you want to know what happened?"

"The boys will be awake in a second. Maybe just a little?"

"Sure." Lucas drank. "I wasn't eighteen. I was twenty-four."

Ava lowered her cup. "What happened when you were twenty-four?"

"Do you really want the details?"

Ava blew on her coffee. "Maybe just a few?"

"My twenty-four-year-old self was pretty messed up."

"I'll bet."

"We talked for a long time."

"For sure."

"He was angry."

"Of course." Ava watched her husband. "Did you explain?"

"Yeah."

"Did you apologize?"

"Yeah."

"Did he forgive you?"

"Yeah, thank God."

"Are you guys okay?"

Lucas shrugged. "We will be." He looked at the boys' bedroom door. "How long did it take you?"

"To get closure?" Ava looked into her cup. "I don't know. Years? My Evil was bad, though. Really bad. It took a long time to forgive myself for letting it happen."

Lucas glanced at his wife. "You killed those girls, didn't you."

"I had to."

"God."

Ava jumped up, spilling coffee on her bathrobe. "Go to hell, Lucas. You have no idea what I went through. If you had to face your Broken-Self in the way mine was damaged you'd kill the whores who did it to you, too. I know you would. I don't need your judgement. The Fix-It bylaw exists so we can find peace, get closure, eliminate the Evil-Makers. It was my right to-"

"Hey." Lucas grabbed his wife's hand. "I'm sorry. My Broken-Self wasn't as hurt as yours. I'm not going to kill my doctor, just sue her for malpractice. I'm sorry."

Ava sniffed. "Thanks." She sank onto the couch, then stared at the brown stain on her robe.

Lucas rubbed her fingers. "Do you want the details about my Evil? You might feel better, knowing we've both faced the truth."

"No." Ava picked up her cup, then gulped down the remaining liquid. "But I'm glad you can do something about yours now."

Grasshoppers chirped in the bushes that lined the retirement complex's garden pathway. The alien ship hovered a foot above the ground as the extraterrestrial helped a frail older woman aboard. Benji and Gael watched the spaceship fly into the sun, then smiled at each other as they reclined on their garden loveseat.

Benji sighed. "It took a long time for Agnes."

Gael nodded. "A long time."

"How old do you think she'll be?"

"Not a clue. Not a single clue."

"That's a lot of past to go through. She must've led a good life."

"Not always. Sometimes it just takes a while for them to find you."

Benji looked at Gael, who was humming a nondescript tune under his breath as he stared at the grasshoppers. Benji poked Gael's shoulder. "Hey. How old were you?"

"Thirty-two."

"What was it?"

"My child died."

"When did you meet your Broken-Self?"

"A couple years later."

"How did you Fix-It?"

Gael shrugged. "Sometimes you can't fix certain hurts."

Benji nodded. He watched the grasshoppers flip their wings and rub their legs together. Their humming resonated in his chest.

Gael started his tuning again, weaving a harmony around the grasshoppers'.

Benji cocked his head. "Want to hear about mine?"

"If you want to share."

"I want to." Benji took a deep breath. "I was forty when the aliens came. They took me on their ship. I waited in the healing chamber and soon after they brought me my Broken-Self. He was fourteen. He looked so small." A grasshopper gave an especially loud hum and Benji smiled, watching it flip its wings. "We talked. I held his hand. He told me what happened to us and-" Benji swallowed. "I cried. He cried. He hugged me. We discussed what I would do."

"What did you do?"

The grasshoppers quieted. Benji took a deep breath. "I burned down my Evil-Maker's house."

Gael nodded. "That's a common one."

"His whole family passed away in the fire."

"Gotta make things right. You gotta make things right."

"I become whole after that day. I got closure." Benji exhaled. "I fixed it."

Gael patted his shoulder. "Yours wasn't the worst. Did you hear about that city up north? A council lady did an Evil to one of the gents and he put poison in the water. Thousands of people gone." He snapped his fingers. "Like that."

"Thanks, Gael." Benji sighed. "That's nice to hear. I don't feel so bad about my own Fix-It."

Gael looked up at the sun. "You haven't... done anything, have you? To upset Agnes?"

"Hells no. I haven't hurt a fly since that day."

"As it should be." Gael nodded. "That's as it should be."

The sun touched the top of the horizon. The grasshoppers hummed as Agnes slowly made her way through the retirement complex's garden. She smiled at Benji and Gael, who'd fallen asleep in each other's arms as the sun set. Agnes removed a spray can of DEET from her purse and made her way over to the bushes. With a focused and thorough spraying she killed the grasshoppers that filled the garden's foliage.

"There." She placed the lid back on the spray can. "That'll teach you for Evil-Making. Damned chirping keeps me up all night. Now I can finally sleep." She smiled. "I needed to Fix-It, real bad."

# VANITY UPRISING

# 10

"Sod it, Addison! We need answers." Addi Peterson, P.I., kicked her standing lamp across her tiny office. The sound of administrative pleasantries filled the registration room outside her open door, drowning out the sharp *ting!* of her light fixture knocking against her partner's filing cabinet. Peterson cracked her knuckles. "And quiet. We need peace and quiet to crack this case."

Her partner, Peter Addison, P.I., righted the overturned standing lamp as he let out a heavy sigh. "I know, I know. I know. We're running out of time. But what can we do? What can we do?"

"I'm at my wit's end, Addison. My wits!" Peterson leaned on her desk, bearing her full weight on her arms as she moaned. "End!" She shook her head, then stared at the desktop. The metal monstrosity took up most of the office and was covered with stacks of files, scribbled notes and week-old shot glasses of espresso. Peterson scrubbed at a coffee stain with her pinky finger, then moaned again. "We have to crack this case—before it's too late."

Addison rested a cheek of his butt on the top of the desk, then twisted to face his partner, grimacing. "Should we review the facts? One more time? Maybe another look-see will show us what we're missing."

A cheerful 'hey, there!' called out across the registration room.

"We could go to the cannabis lounge down the street." Addison scratched his nose. "Get out of this madhouse."

"There's no time. No time!" Peterson whirled around on her Italian steel-toed loafers, then glared through her open office door and into the registry.

She and her P.I. associate, Addison, had moved into the back offices of the Fairfield Motor Association's South Richmond branch out of necessity. In-person meeting spaces were scarce and rent was at an all-time high since the rebellion blew up The Hill. Moving from the luxury tower where she'd run her private investigation firm for thirty years had been a hard call, but with the rebellions persistently upsetting normal life and throwing a wrench in the economy—'conflict inflation forces reformation', she always said—Peterson couldn't afford to have her business burned to the ground like everyone else's. Sharing space with the regional FMA was convenient, and a career-saver, but it was trying. The ongoing car repairs, ticket payments and rental requests being carried out by the clerks in their chipper and upbeat fashion was freakily juxtaposed against her serious P.I. world. And her current case. For example:

"Good morning. How may I help you today?"

"Hello, yes. I'd like to order a licence plate. A personalized licence plate."

"Yes, absolutely. For what reason?"

"It's a graduation gift for my, uh… my daughter. I got her a car and I'd like a fun plate to go with it."

"Certainly. What would you like it to say?"

"Is DONTBL8 available?"

"It is. Oh, that's a good one. I haven't seen that one before."

"Well, my cousin's a bit of a scatterbrain."

"Your cousin?"

"Did I say cousin? I meant daughter. My daughter's a bit of a scatterbrain. I thought this might keep her on track. She's starting at U of SR next semester."

"How adorable."

"Yes. I think my niece will like it there."

"Your niece?"

"Did I say niece? I meant cousin."

"I thought the plate was for your daughter?"

"What did I say the first time?"

"You'd like a personalized licence plate for your daughter's car, which is a graduation gift since she's attending the University of South Richmond this upcoming winter."

"Yes. Is DONTBL8 available?"

"It is. May I see your proof of ownership, some valid insurance, your ID, and a filled in Authorization for Vehicle Services form?"

"Yes, I have them right here. In my purse."

"You're not carrying a purse."

"I meant wallet. My registration documents are in my wallet."

It went on. Mundane trivialities of life played out in the registry while she and P.I. Addison tried to stop the world from coming to an end. Peterson aimed her best withered stare at the nearest FMA clerk, who was happily striking his keyboard with his slender fingers as he loudly extolled the virtues of vanity plates to the entire room, totally unaware of the globe-saving efforts going on in the office behind him. Peterson was tempted to slam her door shut—that should teach him to show some respect for her exalted position— except the September heat was stifling and the airflow in the building piss poor. Instead, she contented herself with an upgraded withered stare that included her speciality: a condemning eyebrow raise. Dismissive glance accomplished, Peterson turned to Addison to resume her daunting, life saving, deserving-of-worship work.

She nodded at Addison, curtly. "There's no time to change location. We'll have to work through these distractions."

"Alrighty. Let's dive in." Addison sighed. "What are the facts? Should we break them down? Point by point?"

"Yes, break them down." Peterson coughed to clear her throat, then shook her head to clear her mind as she did her best to ignore the cheerful clatter of the FMA chippies. She had to focus on her job—her job to save the planet. "Take notes, Addison. We have a duty to record our thoughts as accurately as possible. This sumbitch case is a doozy."

"Yes, siree." Addison grabbed a pad of paper off his desk and started scribbling yet another note to add to the paper littering the desktop.

"Good man." Peterson nodded, then picked up a two-week old espresso shot. Wincing, she swallowed the cold, stale, grainy dregs—'a soft detective loses her perspective', she always said. Wiping her mouth, Peterson flung the shot glass across the office and paced the space, firing off points as Addison scrambled to keep up. "The Roadster Warriors started their campaign to overthrow the government six weeks ago. They razed the parliament building in August and have spread across the country in concentric circles, with Oakland at the epicentre." She gazed at the case chart she'd tacked on her wall, eyes tracing the detailed plotting of the Warriors' rebellious crimes. "We know they're a small group, but extremely powerful. No one has been able to locate and interrogate a single member."

Addison chewed on his tongue as he scribbled. "Roadster Warriors, small but powerful, members unknown." He dotted the 'i', smiled at his pad, then looked up. "Keep going."

"Good morning. How may I help you today?"

"Excuse me, but I'd like to change my licence plate. Switch out my old one for something more kicky and cute."

"Yes, absolutely. What would you like it to say?"

"I'm set on the combo YYC-0803. Is that available?"

"Yes, it is. What kind of vehicle do you currently drive?"

"Oh, just a tiny little thing. An Impala. 2003."

"An older model. Interesting. We don't see many of those, these days. Do you have proof of ownership, valid insurance, your ID-"

Peterson glared at the chipper FMA agent, then turned back to Addison. "Write this down: the Roadster Warriors have been meeting every week to plan their attacks, then they burn down another government building a few days later."

"Attacks follow meetings." Addison frowned. "There was some kind of order to it, wasn't there?"

"There most certainly was, Pete m'lad." Peterson pressed her thumb into the case chart, pinning a tracking document to the wall. "They occur at weekly intervals. The Warrior's meetings happen on Saturdays, then the attacks happen the following Tuesday or Wednesday." Peterson frowned. "Like clockwork."

"European clockwork."

"Swiss European clockwork." Peterson pressed her nose into the case chart, trying to glean some meaning from the swirls looping the paper. "Extremely efficient clockwork."

"And nobody has been able to locate them." Addison shook his head. "Kind of embarrassing for the local police, eh?"

"Good morning. How may I help you today?"

"Hey. I wanna order a custom license plate. For my motorcycle."

"Yes, absolutely. For what reason?"

"Dunno. Wanna mix it up. That okay with you?"

"Certainly. Who doesn't like a fresh start? What would you like your plate to say?"

"YEG-0810."

"Oh, gosh. I'm sorry. For motorcycle plates, you can only use five spaces."

"Just five? Shit, that doesn't work."

"This is a profanity-free environment, ma'am. Is there another combination you'd like instead?"

"I'll have to think about it. Shit. Shit on a pancake. I'll have to come back later. Fuck. Fuck on a-"

"Thank you for your business. When you return, please remember that here at the Fairfield Motor Association we conduct our business with professional civility."

Peterson shook her head, trying to erase the voice of the clattering agent. "Sorry, Addison, old boy. What was that?"

"It's embarrassing." Addison grinned. "For the police."

"Embarrassing is right." Peterson cracked her knuckles. "But we can't be too hard on public servants. These Roadster Warriors are next level. Next level!"

"What else do we know?" Addison looked down at his pad, pencil at the ready. "What are the other facts of the case?"

"Each meeting takes place in a different Fairfieldian city. The Warriors have some way of moving around the province that no one has been able to track, which makes them extremely elusive."

"And sneaky." Addison scribbled. "Extremely sneaky."

"Right. So they move around the province, week by week, meeting then attacking, meeting then attacking." Peterson kicked her filing cabinet—'steel-toed shoes avoid a bruise', she always said. "We have no way to anticipate what the Warrior's next meeting spot will be. We have no way to catch one of them."

"Good morning. How may I help you today?"

"Hey, um. I'd like to register a vehicle? A new vehicle?"

"Yes, absolutely. What kind of vehicle?"

"Um, uh. A tractor-trailer?"

"Certainly. May I have your proof of ownership, valid insurance, your-"

"Um, uh. Um, can I get a personalized licence plate? Um. Can I get a speciality licence plate?"

"Certainly. What would you like it to say?"

"Um, uh. YMM-0817?"

"Yes, that is available. Can I see your proof of ownership, valid insurance, ID and Authorization for Vehicle Services form?"

"Uh, yeah. I have those right here?"

"Thank you. Now, don't forget that on a tractor-trailer your licence plate must be attached to the front of your vehicle-"

Peterson moved to shut her door, then stopped. Beads of sweat trickled down the sides of poor Addison's face and his nose was maple leaf red. Instead of putting her partner through increased stuffy suffering, Peterson frowned harder at the back of the clerk's head—a more withering stare. This one included a suggestive frown.

Sweaty Addison shifted on the desk, moving from one ass cheek to the other. "What else do we know? About the Roadster Warrior rebellion?"

"We know that they're communicating in secret." Peterson cracked her neck. "Through some unknown method."

"Right, right. Right. Secret. Unknown. Concealed."

"Yes." Peterson shut her eyes, sensing an oncoming headache. "And other similar synonyms."

Addison scribbled on his pad. "The cops checked out all the usual chat forums, but there's nothing. Right? Right? Not online, not through Canuckia Post, not by carrier magpie." He looked up. "These dissenters are diabolical. Right?"

"Extremely diabolical." Peterson nodded. The back of her skull throbbed. "I spoke with the United Canuckian Codebreaker Coalition and they haven't found anything. We've got no leads on this." Her eyelids flew open and she banged her fist on the desk. "No leads!"

"Good afternoon. How may I help you today?"

"I'd like to purchase a vanity licence plate for my vehicle. Looking to do a little upgrade, if you know what I mean."

"Yes, absolutely. What would you like on your plate?"

"Do you have PB4UG0? I saw a version of that slogan when I was in the States last summer and I was tickled, if you know what I mean. I've been wanting my own plate ever since. Is it okay to use only six spaces? If you know what I mean?"

"What kind of vehicle do you have?"

"A midsized two door."

"Make and model?"

"Oh, ha! A 2025 Chevy Cavalier."

"I wasn't aware Chevrolet continued that model beyond 2014."

"Oh, ha! I got it in Germany. My sister has connections with a car factory owner over there, if you know what I-"

"Certainly. For a four-door Cavalier, six spaces is absolutely acceptable."

"Oh. Ha!"

"May I see your proof of ownership-"

"Addi?"

Peterson looked back at her partner. "Sorry. Distracted. Gal'derned agents. What did you say?"

"I asked about the morale boosters." Addison frowned. "Any new info about how the Roadsters are keeping spirits so high?"

"Nothing new." Peterson leaned her forehead against the case chart. "Typically within these groups of aggressive activists someone gets scared and starts making mistakes. But everything we know about the Roadsters tells us that they're happy, thriving and intent on Canuckian domination. They've taken over every eastern province as they've swept towards the west—without breaking a sweat!" She pulled a tissue out from a nearby box and flung it at Addison, who gratefully mopped his dripping brow. Peterson shook her head, moaning. "It's not right."

"It's weird, is what it is." Addison tucked the tissue up his sleeve, then resumed his tongue-biting scribbles. "Right weird. How are they staying so focused? So cheerful?"

"Haze it, Addison!" Peterson cracked her ribcage. "As concerning as Warrior morale is, I'm still hellbent on finding out how they're passing along their secret messages. If we can figure that out, we can break the link—decipher their code and find out where their next meeting will be. And when."

"Good afternoon. How may I help you today?"

"Hey. I'd like a vanity plate. I drive a Ford Focus. I want YZU-0824."

"Yes, certainly. May I see your-"

"Fog it, Addison!" Peterson kicked her desk. "We're running out of time! There's only a finite number of government buildings left in Fairfield!"

"And once the Roadsters burn them all, they'll move on to the last province."

"Then they'll have control over the whole country."

"Then they'll move onto the next country. And the next."

"Then they'll have control over the whole continent."

"Then they'll move onto the next continent. And the next."

"Then they'll have control over the whole world!" Peterson slumped over her desk. "The stakes are high and everyone is counting on us. On us! We have to crack this case!"

"Good afternoon. How may I help you today?"

"Hi! How are you?"

"Me? Oh, I'm dandy. Thank you. What can I do for you?"

"I'm here because I'd like to purchase a personalized plate. Or, switch out my plate. You know, replace my plate with a new one. An interesting one. A plate that says interesting things instead of normal licensing codes and stuff."

"Do you mean a specialty plate?"

"Nooooo…"

"A vanity plate?"

"Yes! That's it, a vanity plate. I'm here to get a vanity plate, please. To replace my old plate."

"Yes, absolutely. What kind of vehicle do you drive?"

"Oh, I don't drive. I ride."

"Beg pardon?"

"My vehicle is a scooter. An electric scooter."

"I'm sorry, but electric scooters are ineligible for licence plates."

"Oh. Okay. Well, can I get a, uh… what did you call it?"

"A vanity plate?"

"Yes, a vanity plate. Can I get a vanity plate for my other vehicle?"

"Yes, certainly. What type of vehicle is that?"

"A backhoe."

"Excuse me?"

"You know, a backhoe. One of those diggy, scoopy, arm diggy diggers. With the wheels. And the cabin and stuff."

"You drive a backhoe?"

"When I'm not using my scooter, yes."

"On city roads?"

"No, on my farm."

"Oh, thank goodness. Unfortunately, backhoes are ineligible for vanity plates."

"Oh. Crap!"

"This is a profanity-free environment, miss."

"Oh. Cucumbers! Well, what about my other vehicle?"

"Your other vehicle?"

"Yes. I also drive a golf cart."

"I'm sorry, but golf carts are ineligible for vanity-"

"Pickled cucumbers! Which vehicles are allowed to have... um, what did you call them?"

"Vanity plates."

"Yeah, which vehicles are allowed to have vanity plates?"

"Do you own a car?"

"Maybe."

"You could get a vanity plate for a car."

"Why didn't you say that in the first place? I'd like a vanity plate for my car, please."

"Certainly. What would you like your vanity plate to say?"

"YXH-0831."

"Certainly. May I see your-"

"Hey, Peterson? Peterson?" Addison's voice invaded Peterson's fuddle-duddled thoughts. "Peterson? Hey, Peterson?"

"Yes, man? What is it?" Peterson turned away from the registration room and back to her partner. "Spit it out!"

"I had an idea." Addison thrust the pad into Peterson's hands. "What if the code—the way the Roadsters are communicating and keeping up morale—what if the code was through some kind of inter-connected provincial network? Something that ran the length and breadth of the province? Of the country? Something that tied everything together? Everyone together!"

"Now you're talking!" Peterson slapped her hands together. "What are you thinking?"

"What if-" Addison paused and his eyes lit up. "This is a little out there, but stay with me. What if the Roadster Warriors are sending messages through Snapchat? You know, quick pics that disappear after you read them? There'd be no evidence of their trail. It's brilliant!"

Peterson smacked Addison upside the head. "You doofus. Don't you think Snapchat was the first place the UCCC looked?" She shook her tingling palm—Addison's head was rock hard. "Hoof it, Peter. Nobody gets away with online conspiracy anymore. Nobody!"

Addison rubbed the back of his boulder. "Gosh, I'm sorry. I just thought-"

"Well, you thought wrong." Peterson shoved the pad back into Addison's hands. "Think again."

"Hmmmmm." Addison started scribbling. "Give me one sec. One secondy sec."

"Good evening. How may I help you today?"

"Hello."

"Hello. How can I help you?"

"I'd like to upgrade my licence plate."

"Absolutely. What can I get for you?"

"I'd like a North Richmond Gassers plate."

"I'm sorry. After their outstanding playoff run, we're all out of Gassers plates."

"Oh. Then I'd like a South Richmond Sparks plate."

"I'm sorry. After their outstanding playoff run, we're all out of Sparks plates."

"Oh. Then I'd like a Support Our Troops plate."

"I'm sorry. After Canuckia's outstanding World War IV run, we're all out of Support Our Troops plates."

"Oh. Then I'd like a Veteran's plate."

"Are you a veteran?"

"…yes."

"Certainly. If you show me your proof of ownership, valid insurance and your ID, I can make the transfer. You'll receive your new plate in six to eight weeks."

"One more thing. Can I get it a little sooner? Before Saturday?"

"Yes, absolutely. For a small fee, FMA can ship you your new plate tomorrow."

"One more thing. Can my new plate be a vanity plate?"

"Yes, absolutely. What would you like it to say?"

"YQU-0907."

"I'm sorry, that plate is already taken."

"Oh. How about BR3ADY?"

"Yes, BR3ADY is available."

"Hey!" Addison looked up. "I think—I think I got something!"

"What is it, man?" Peterson hurried to her partner's side. "Shoot it out, Pete!"

"Look at this." He waved the pad in Peterson's face. "I just realized—the UCCC have been unsuccessful at tracking the Roadsters and the local police have been unsuccessful at tracking the Roadsters—but the Roadsters don't know about us! They don't know about Addi Peterson and Peter Addison!"

Peterson looked up, eyes wide. "By golly, you're right! You did it, Addison! You did it! You saved the case!"

"I did!" Addison wiggled around the office, clicking his heels together as he danced a merry jig. "I did do it!"

"With our P.I. anonymity, we have the element of surprise." Peterson rubbed her hands together. "Law enforcement has been too public about all this—in the media, on the Canuckian alert network and over the World Wide Press. The Roadsters know the government is coming for them, but they don't know about us. They don't know about Addi and Pete, Pete and Addi. We'll get them. We'll get them, yet!"

"We'll get them, because they don't know we're on their trail!"

"The Warriors have no idea that Prime Minister Bublé hired us to crack the code."

"We'll crack the code, because they won't see us coming!"

"The Warriors have no idea our brilliant P.I. firm is closing in on their whereabouts."

"We're closing in on their whereabouts, because they don't know we exist!"

"The Warriors have no idea that P.I. Addi and Peter are going to stick it to 'em." She grinned. "Stick it to 'em, good."

"Yes!" Addison slid to the floor, then leaned back on his knees as he riffed on an air guitar.

"Let's get back to work." Peterson hoisted her partner to his feet, then threw the pad in his face. "Now that we know we have the element of surprise, we can take our time. Go through the details. Start at the beginning, Addison, then sum it up. What are the facts?"

"The Roadster Warriors started their campaign six weeks ago, they meet in different locations around the province every Saturday, they burn down a different government building midweek, they communicate by a secret code, and their morale is extremely high." Addison looked up. "Am I missing anything?"

"Sounds good to me." Peterson beamed. "And don't forget to write down that we have the element of surprise.

Element. Of. Surprise. Got it? Our anonymity gives us power. And with that power, we will save the world."

"Right." Addison scribbled on his pad. "Power comes from secrecy… anonymity… concealment."

"Yes." Peterson grinned, her headache rapidly disappearing. "And other similar synonyms."

"Good evening. How may I help you today?"

"Good evening. I'd like to buy a vanity licence plate for my Hyundai EV."

"Yes, absolutely. Do you know what you'd like it to say?"

"I do. FKADDINPETER."

"I'm sorry, that has too many letters."

"Oh. What about, EATSHTPI?"

"You need a number, sir."

"EATSHTP1?"

"That has too many letters, sir."

"Oh. P1SRDCKS?"

"That one is taken, sir."

"Oh. What about P1SRDX?"

"That one is available."

"Hold on, no. Can it be, P1S-RDX? With a space?"

"A space, sir?"

"Yes, a space. Between P1S and RDX."

"So, P-1-S, space, R-D-X?"

"Yes, please. So it reads, P1, plural, space, are DX."

"Let me run it through our system."

"If that's not available, I'm also willing to take RDWR4LF."

"One moment, sir."

"Thank you."

"Alright. It looks as though your preferred choice is available."

"P1S, space, RDX?"

"Yes, P1S-RDX. The Fairfield Motor Association can put that on a plate for you."

"Thank you so much. I really appreciate this."

"Our pleasure, sir."

"Excellent."

"If you can show me your proof of vehicle ownership, your valid insurance, your identification, your completed Authorization of Vehicle Services form and give me your mailing address, I can have that plate sent to you in six to eight weeks."

"Any way I can get a rush on that?"

"Certainly. For a small fee, FMA can ship you your new vanity plate tomorrow."

"Excellent. I need it for a small gathering this Saturday."

"How delightful. Anything else I can do for you this evening?"

"No, that's all I need. Thanks again for passing on this information. It's been morale boosting."

Peterson tore her eyes away from the chipper FMA clerk as he started packing up his desk, ready to head home. She smirked at the emptying registry, employed with agents who were living their mediocre lives and plodding through their administrative dalliances, unaware of the P.I. brilliance that was saving the planet in their back offices. The chipper agent flicked off the lights as the workday officially ended and he and the rest of the clerks exited the registry, locking the main door behind them.

Peterson turned to her partner of thirty years and chuckled. "Finally. No more distractions, Addison." She clapped her P.I. associate on the back. "Now that we have some peace and quiet, we can crack this case."

# PREDATOR

# 11

Lies were told in days of old
That never once were spread
But in an age where truth is staged
Deceit leaves pure hearts dead.

Choices made can break or aid
In shaping youthful dreams
But digital forums with loosened decorums
Will tear them apart at the seams.

Within a chatroom Our Girl met her doom
By starting a dangerous journey:
A drunken call cursed that led to a hearse
And Our Femme carried off on a gurney.

If she had been told that her fate would unfold

After living her whole life onscreen

She might have refrained, or even abstained,

From chugging that triple Jim Beam,

But let's start at the top of our scene.


On a fresh, clear day at the end of May

Our Heroine settled down

To scroll her posts and comment the most

Of everyone in her town.


Our Lady was young, determined and fun,

A beauty on everyone's phone.

Her handle said "Love" and her pic was a dove

And her filter was sepia tone.


This youthful sprite stayed up that night

Scanning, then hating, the news.

Love shared her opinions with millions of minions

While downing a sixer of booze.


The world was a mess, friends under duress,

And she had to help them all thrive.

Love tweeted and snapped, then cyber bitch-slapped—

What a time to be alive!

She had just turned twenty-five.


The hours ticked by and stars stained the sky

As Love pursued her goals—

To enlighten and lift with fortuitous thrift

While combating the cringey-caked trolls.


With a hollow ting and an epic ring

Her cell began to buzz.

Love didn't linger, she flicked her finger

And answered—as everyone does.


A stranger's face, set back apace,

Appeared on her Samsung screen.

It was a fellow whose vibe was mellow

With cheekbones both lithe and lean.


Love called out, "Hello?" He answered, "You know,

"I've been liking you every day.

"I'm awestruck, my dear, by your Instagram sneer

"And I want you to be my bae."

Love shook her head, then quietly said,

"My parents would never allow it.

"But if you give a reason I'll ditch them this season

"So we can match up and then plough it."

The stranger smiled, then said, "I'm beguiled.

"I've never known someone so strong.

"If you can break loose from your parental noose

"I'd 'Love' us to marry lifelong."

Our Girl gave a squeal with a drunken peal

Of glee—she had found her true match!

She nodded with joy, then said, "You're the boy

"I've simply been dying to catch.

"I'll meet you tonight by the blue moonlight

"In the parking lot down by the lake.

"Just come in your car so I know who you are—

"I don't want to be played by a fake."

The stranger smirked. His eyebrow twerked.

He said, "I can be there in ten."

Love's phone seemed to spark before it went dark

But she let out a squeal again.


Love jumped to her feet, then quickly and neat

She packed her belongings in bags.

On tiptoe she scurried, unworried, though hurried—

Oblivious to the red flags;

The warnings attached to his tags.


When Love arrived at the parking lot drive

Her stranger was nowhere around.

She patiently waited and anticipated

The lit life she'd finally found.


But minutes ticked by. Love let out a sigh

And said, "Did my guy fall asleep?"

Then a flash of white light lit up the midnight

As the stranger arrived in his Jeep.

Love clapped her hands, then ran to her man
And hopped in the back of his auto.
His wheels gave a screech that drowned out all speech
As the Jeep spun away with bravado.

The dust in the lot encircled the spot
Where Love had so recently stood.
Her cell lay discarded, though once she had guarded
The tech with determined sainthood.

On that evening in spring Love's phone gave a ring:
Her parents had noticed her gone
But their bright brilliant child, so happy and wild,
Was off with the techie Don Juan.

The cell rang and rang. The clamouring sang
Through the lot—the phone lost out of sight—
So a couple bereft was all that was left
Of the lovely girl stolen that night.
A sin that would not be made right.

Lies were told in days of old
That never once were spread,
But in an age where truths are staged
Deceit leaves pure hearts dead.

When wolves traverse the virtual 'verse,
Hunting, then trapping, their prey
It takes tenacity and pugnacity
To avoid foul play.

If Love had been taught that her choices were fraught
With malevolent paths to cremation
She might have been spared—or else, more prepared
When her socials sent notifications.

But Love, on her screen, was a self-righteous Queen
Impervious to other's wrath.
So she answered a call and that was all it took

For a sociopath.

# DUKE KETTER

# AND THE MOUNTAIN OF DRAGONS

# 12

A goblin chops off my head.

"Zap!" I throw the gaming controller across the basement den. It bounces off the frame of Bav's TV and lands on her disco rug. I push myself out of the couch and stomp over to the foot of the stairs. The room flickers. I scratch my temple. The flickering stops. "Bav! I'm going out!"

"No, you are not! You didn't do the dishes!"

"I'll do them later!"

"Get your ass upstairs! Going out is a privilege, not a right! And stop calling me Bav! I'm your mother, for chrissakes!"

"Chosen mother." As I trudge up the stairs I mutter everything I wish I could say to Bav under my breath.

Bav sits at the kitchen table smoking a joint—her third one that afternoon. She grins at me with her brownish teeth and gestures to the sink. "Wash up. Then you can go out."

I glare at the heaping pile of dishes. They haven't been touched in days. "We have a dishwasher, Bav."

"Washing them by hand builds character. My mother did everything for me and I was a loser when I finally moved out of her house. Life is hard, kid. You should thank me for preparing you for it."

I grit my teeth as I stomp over to the sink. "Thanks, Bav."

She jumps off her stool and thwacks the back of my head. "Mom."

"Ow! Geez. Mom."

Bav's cellphone rings. She brightens as she looks at her screen. "Oh, good. I've been waiting for her to call me back." She holds her phone to her ear. "Daeny! Where you at, girl?" Bav slinks out of the kitchen, hissing at me as she leaves. "Those had better be finished by the time I'm done this call. And don't forget to take out the garbage. It's starting to—Giiirl! He did what?"

The bell hanging over the door tinkles as I push it open and stomp into Flagnad's Video Game Emporium. A neon sign buzzes in the store's window, blinking its daily advertisements. That afternoon it proclaimed the benefits of probiotic vitamins: great skin, long nails, thick hair. Stupid product. I snort as I pass the sign.

Bella Goose—the Emporium's cute assistant manager—looks up from her phone and beams as I approach the checkout counter. "Hiya, Duke. How's Dragon Mountain going?"

"I keep getting killed on level 555."

"Big goblin with the double-sided axe?"

I shrug.

Bella chuckles, then tucks her chestnut-coloured hair behind her ear—she draws attention to her newest hairstyle whenever she can. "Are you too tense when you play? In Dragon Mountain you have to relax into the game, not try to control it."

"I don't need a lecture about my acceptance issues, Bel."

Bella smiles. "I'm just trying to say, don't think about it too hard. But Jon can show you the hack for level 555 if you want."

I kick the counter's baseboard with the toe of my sneaker. "I don't want to cheat again."

"It's not cheating. Jon doesn't mind. No one's been in today, so-"

"Miss Goose?"

Bella pales, then whirls around. A figure stands in the doorway of the manager's office, hovering in shadow, still and staring. Bella's shoulders tense. "It's Duke. Duke's having trouble with level 555 of Dragon Mountain."

"I told you that game was a waste of time." The figure steps over the doorway's threshold. The light from the window display casts a red glow over his silvered hair, making him look like a strawberry. The man shoots me a wry smile as he joins Bella behind the counter. "How's your mother, Duke?"

"Same." I stare at the floor. The tile is filthy—Jon Sleet, the Emporium's surly shift supervisor, avoids mopping whenever he can. I run my sneaker toe through the dirt. "Don't worry. I escaped without too much damage."

The silver-haired man makes a sound, a rasp. "Vacuuming again?"

"Dishes."

"Ah." The man taps the counter. I look up. Silver-haired Flagnad, the store's elderly owner, leans toward me. "You know, I have something better than Dragon Mountain." Bella inhales sharply. Flagnad raises his hand, silencing her. "Duke? You're too talented to waste your time with these cheap modern systems. Let me show you the real deal."

I frown. Flagnad pretends to be mystical whenever he can—it's part of what makes the Emporium so popular. He knows his audience and he plays them well. Not me, though. I'm smarter than most gamers. I shrug. "Jon can show me how to defeat the big goblin."

Flagnad lowers his hand and his smile quirks. "Let me know how that goes." He slowly spins on his heel, then disappears into the shadows of his office.

Bella exhales, then nods toward the storage room. "Jon's in the back. It's stock day."

"Thanks." I wind my way through shelves of D&D books, dice and figurines, then duck under the rack that displays Flagnad's movie props—all for sale at a very reasonable price that in no way takes advantage of the geeks and dreamers willing to shell out anything for a piece of their hero's junk.

Fools.

I stomp into the storage room. Jon's unloading boxes and typing serial codes into the store's desktop.

I sigh. "Hey, Sleet."

Jon grunts. "Busy right now. Come back later."

"I need you, Sleet. I need your help."

"I'm busy, Duke. Unlike you, I have to focus when I'm doing number stuff."

I stomp over and help him unload, pulling puzzles and anime stuffed creatures from the nearest crate and placing them on the shelves. I wave a furry bird thing in Jon's face. "What the heck? Nad sell out?"

"No." Jon frowns at his computer screen, typing with concentration. "Flagnad wants to keep me and Bella fed and watered. He makes more money when he sells collectibles. He gives us that money. Bella and me don't die." His eyes dart towards me, then back to the screen. "Not all of us are seventeen and living the good life with mommy."

"She's not my mother."

"She's better than nothing." Jon sighs. He massages his neck. "Doesn't matter. It's not like any of this is real."

"Okay, great." I throw the furry bird thing on the shelf. "Bella says you know how to get past level 555 in Dragon Mountain. Can you show me?"

"Sure." Jon smirks. "For fifty bucks."

"You know I don't have that." I stamp my foot. "Come on, just show me the hack."

"Sixty bucks."

"Sleet, don't be a dweeb. You do this every time. We haggle for days and you end up showing me for free, anyway. Can't we skip the middle and get to the end where I level up?"

"The middle is where you level up, Duke."

"Cut the cryptic shit and show me the hack."

Jon laughs. "Fine. Come back here after we close—if you can escape Mommy Dearest—and I'll walk you through it. Bring your controller. You jammed the buttons on mine and I had to get a new one."

"That's not true."

"Just bring it." Jon frowns. He reaches into his pocket and removes a small white bottle—painkillers. He untwists the top and pops two of the liquid capsules into his mouth, wincing as he swallows. "These things always get stuck on the way down."

"That's what water's for."

"See you at closing, Duke." Jon hunches over his keyboard. "Or not, I don't care. It's not like any of this matters."

I stomp out of the storage room and head for the Emporium's exit. As I pass the highest tower of board games Bella jumps out from behind the stack. "Hiya, Duke."

"Frickin' A, Bel!" I clutch my chest. "You almost killed me."

Bella tucks her hair behind her ears, then thrusts a folded envelope into my hands. "Take this."

I glare at the envelope. "What is it?"

"Just take it." Bella steps back. "Read it outside, okay?"

"Bella-"

"I have to go." Bella turns, then jogs towards the counter.

I sigh, then push open the front door. The tinkling of the bell follows me as I step onto the Old York City sidewalk. I open the envelope and pull out a crumpled piece of paper. Slanted writing crawls across its surface.

I tilt my head to read it.

Within the Park Aboard the Train
A Journey to Escape the Reign
of Holy Mother, Cruel and Strong
A Trip you'll take to Right your Wrong

You feel a Captive, Weakly Dim,
but take the Quest and follow Him
to Best the Monsters, Sort the Trash
and Mow the Field to Find the Cache

She Sits and Broods and Breeds the Beasts
and Only You are Her Release
so Join the Allies, Weather Storms,
your Final Prize is Duke Reborn

Tomorrow when the Clock Strikes Three
come Join Us at the Twisted Tree
Leave All Behind, You Are Enough,
but be Prepared, this Journey's Tough

You've Lived Alone, Trapped in your Head

so Small you might as well be Dead

but Join the Fight and Be Set Free—

Life Is Our Most Precious Commodity


I glare at the poem. I crumple the page in my hand, huck the wad of paper in the city recycling bin, then shove my hands in my pockets—heading for home. "Final stanza didn't even work."


A troll stabs me in the belly.

"Zap!" I throw the gaming controller across the den. It bounces off the side of Bav's poker table and lands on her drinking hammock. The back of my head throbs. I massage my neck, trying to ease the tension.

Bav slinks down the stairs, sipping a soda.

I glare at her. "What is that?"

"This is an ice cold can of Pepsi-Cola." Bav takes a slug of the drink, then jiggles the soda in my face. "Want some?"

"Gross. Germs."

Bav slurps loudly, then belches. She points at the gaming controller. "Can you not wreck all my stuff?"

"Sorry." The room shimmers. I rub my temple. The shimmering stops. "I can't beat this level."

"I thought Jon was supposed to show you how, last night."

"He wasn't there."

Bav smirks, then slurps her Pepsi. "That's what you get for running off when you have chores to do." She sits on the arm of the couch, then slurps again. "Karma, baby."

"I did my chores."

"Yeah, after you got back from your mid-day misdeeds." Bav runs her long nails through my hair. I scoot to the far side of the sofa, away from her. She laughs. "Kid, life is going to eat you up and spit you out if you can't handle a little affection." She picks up the controller and tosses it at me. "You know what they say. Losers always quit, and quitters never level up."

"I don't think anyone has said that ever."

The doorbell rings.

"God, I hope that's Micheal B. Jordan." Bav crushes the Pepsi can, then tosses it in the darkest corner of the basement as she slinks up the stairs. "I've been tweeting him for months, begging him to rescue me from this Dark

Dimension. FYI—sink's full again. It takes a lot of dishes to make eggs benedick."

"Eggs Benedict!" Bav disappears into the kitchen. I holler after her. "And you didn't make eggs Benedict! Scrambling an egg on a piece of toast doesn't count as-"

"Duke?"

A silver-haired figure hovers in the doorway. Flagnad floats down the staircase, then hovers in the middle of the den. He looks around the room—at the sparkly disco rug, hemp drinking hammock, dingy television set, chipped foosball table and rickety vacuum from 1950 that leans against a fake potted plant. He places his hand on Bav's purple poker table. "Classy."

I push myself out of the couch. "What are you doing here?"

"You dropped this." Flagnad holds out his hand. Clutched in his fingers is the poem—crumbled, a little torn, but definitely the poem.

I stare. "I threw that away."

"You dropped it."

"I wadded it into a tiny ball and recycled it."

"How very responsible of you." Flagnad smiles, misty and vague. "Except you didn't throw it away. Bella found it on the sidewalk outside the store this morning." He waves the page back and forth. "It has your name on it."

"What?" I grab the paper, then smooth it out on top of Bav's jukebox. There it is—my name, scrawled on the backside of the poem:

D. KETTER
The Gaming Den in the Basement
1954 Fifth Avenue
Centreville, OY

Flagnad nods, spooky and slow. "Seems like it's meant for you, doesn't it."

"Did you write this?" I shake the poem in his face. "I told you, I'm not interested in your real-life adventure fantasies. I'm not naive, or easy prey for an old perv."

"I've never once thought you were naive." Flagnad floats across the room and up the stairs. At the top he pauses, then stares down at me. "Young, perhaps. Scared? Definitely. But naive?" He shakes his silver head. "No, not you. Not Duke Ketter. Duke Ketter's too smart to waste time staying stuck in a basement." He turns. His voice floats down the stairs as he floats into the kitchen. "See you at three."

Hands shoved in my pockets I stand under the ugliest Elm in Centric Park. Taxis and Ubers honk and beak as they drive bumper to bumper past the park, their roof LED displays glittering in the sun. My eye lingers on a particularly spicy advertisement for Personal Relaxation Relationships—only $200 an hour to connect with a decent human—but after the taxi drives away I drag my attention back into Centric. And back onto the ugly Elm.

Stupid tree.

Balancing on the tips of my sneakers, I mutter, "Where the hell are you, old ma-"

"Hiya, Duke."

Bella steps out from behind the Elm and I jump. "Stop that! I'm going to have a heart attack."

She smiles, tucking her hair behind her ears. "I'm glad you came. I didn't want to do this alone."

I nudge an anthill with my shoe. Insects spill out of the mound, furious. I snicker, then stare into Bella's chestnut-coloured eyes. "What are you doing here?"

"Flagnad." Bella shrugs. "He closed the Emporium and told me to meet you here. Someone sent me a poem, too."

The sound of rustling leaves fills the park. We look around. Centric is empty—deserted. Bella wrinkles her nose and her freckles disappear in the folds. She turns towards the Elm, then her eyes flicker up into the tree. "Did you hear that?"

I follow her gaze into the branches above us. There's a loud *crack!* and amid a shower of leaves a huge bird descends right on top of our heads.

Bella shrieks. I leap between her and the giant flyer. "Shoo!" I wave my arms. The bird flaps its wings, then settles on a tree root. I wave my arms again. "Get away, bird!"

The bird blinks its leathery eyelids. Bella hides behind me, holding onto my belt. The bird cocks its head to the side, then opens its beak. "Looks like a tornado's on the way."

I gasp. Bella's hands quiver on my waist.

"Ominous warning, tornados." The bird chirps. "They herald new beginnings."

I wave my arms. "Get away from us, bird!"

The bird hops back, then chirps again. "I'm an eagle."

"You're an abomination. Get away from us!"

The bird clucks its tongue. "How would you like it if I called you Duck? And her, Stella?" The bird cocks its head towards the sky and opens its beak. "Stellaaaaaaa!" It looks down, grinning. "Has a nice ring to it, but that doesn't make it right."

"What the zap are you?"

"Her name is Goat." Flagnad steps around the Elm. He hands Bella and me suitcases—one for each of us—then adjusts the lapels on his khaki-green jacket. "Goat? Meet Duke and Bella. Duke and Bella? Meet Goat. Goat will be joining us on our journey."

"I had to come along." The bird chirps. "You wouldn't want to get stuck in the quagmires of Kepler-186f again, would you? Flagnad?"

"I was the one who saved you from the quagmires, Goat."

"You were the one who pushed me into the quagmires, then fell in after me. If it wasn't for my quick flapping-"

I raise my hand. "I changed my mind. I don't want to do this anymore."

"Don't go." Bella clutches my arm. "You can't leave me alone with them."

"Goat's harmless." Flagnad tickles the bird's chin. Its eyelids close and it chirps with pleasure. Flagnad chuckles. "She's just like you."

"Talking birds are not like me. I'm leaving, right now."

"Duke!"

"Don't abandon Bella, Duke." Flagnad's voice rasps, wispy and brooding. "Prove you're worthy of this gift."

I glare at Flagnad, glare at the bird, then spin around to face Bella. "If that thing tries to peck me, I'm gone."

She nods, then releases my belt. "Deal." Bella sighs, massaging the back of her neck with her suitcase-free hand. "Where's the train, Flagnad?"

"Step back, children." Flagnad gestures to the tree trunk. "It'll be here within the merest of moments."

We step away from the Elm. The bird hops beside us, flexing its huge talons. "Is Jon joining the rebellion?"

Flagnad stares at the trunk, subdued and stagnant. He reaches into his shoulder satchel and removes a fish—its red scales catch the Centric Park light, sparkling and strawberry-coloured. Flagnad tosses the herring to the bird. "Not this time."

The bird opens its beak, snatches the fish from the air, then swallows it whole. It cocks its head. "You have to cancel out the idiom with a logical fallacy for the message to be effective."

Flagnad removes a second fish from his satchel, then tosses it to the bird.

The bird swallows the second herring whole, then grins. "We're all going to die someday."

Bella grabs my arm and whispers in my ear. "Jon didn't show up for his shift this morning. I have a bad feeling about thi-"

A train whistle pierces the air, breaking the silence that fills Centric Park. The Elm splits in two and we scramble away as a train engine bursts from the trunk. The steamer chugs over the Elm's roots and down a park path, smokestack puffing and wheel axles churning as it turns abruptly, pulling up beside us. It groans to a halt and the dining car door flies open. The bird hops onto the bottom step, its right eye glaring. "Better climb aboard before society collapses."

Flagnad chuckles and follows the bird onto the train. Bella hoists her suitcase over her shoulder, then climbs after them. I sigh, take one last look at Old York City, then jump on the step as the train's engine roars and the steamer starts puffing. As I hurtle up the steps and into the dining car the door slams shut. We travel into the tree—and beyond. Through the door's fogged window I watch the woody gateway seal behind us. Bella gasps and I turn, holding my suitcase tight against my hip. She points outside. I stare in awe.

Field after field of lush green landscape chugs by on either side of the train. Purple mountains topped with snow sparkle in the distance. Towering emerald trees and deep blue lakes dot the hillside. Burnt-brown desert sands line the aquamarine oceans to our left and leafy, buzzing rainforests crowd the skyline to our right. I gape in wonder, taking it all in.

Flagnad raises his arms. "Welcome to Coalshaft, my friends."

Something taps my shoulder. "Interesting to be in a world outside of total government control, isn't it."

The bird's beak juts in my face. I yell and leap back, into the aisle and away from the threatening aviator.

"Frak!"

I spin around. In my hurry to get away from Goat I've smacked into a girl. A girl with large ochre eyes and toffee-scented hair. She pushes me and I stumble into Bella. I blush, lifting my fingers in apology. "I didn't see you."

"No kidding." The girl shakes out her golden locks, then turns her fiery-black gaze on me. "Not the best start to a partnership. If we don't work together, we'll die alone."

"What?"

Flagnad smiles, floating forward and placing his hand on the girl's shoulder. "Meet your travelling companions. Duke? Bella? This is Tuffy. And that-" He points to a tiny male huddled in a booth. "-is Anigo. They received poems as well." Flagnad grins. "You will all be reborn together."

Goat clucks. "If you make it to the end, of course."

A loud roar fills the dining car. The tiny male—Anigo—whimpers in his booth.

Bella spins in a circle, eyes wide. "What was that?"

Flagnad smiles. "That, my friends, is your initiation." He points at the trolley. Giant stony shapes lumber towards us, roaring as they shove their way up the aisle. "Trolls."

Tuffy grins. "They don't look scary to me."

Flagnad smiles and floats backwards. "Then let's see what you're made of."

The trolls burst into the dining car, smashing through the door that joins the train compartments. The huge beasts snarl, then begin ripping up booths and throwing them aside like they were sticks.

Goat takes off, flying above our heads and clucking her support. "There's only two of them. They're weak. Trolls are the byproduct of humanity raised under an oppressive system that perpetuates poverty of the masses, inequity in education and physiological injustice for the working class."

"What the deuce does that mean, Goat?"

"They're easy to kill, Duke."

"We have to kill them?" Bella hides behind Flagnad. "That wasn't in the poem."

The tiny male scampers over, cowering behind me. Tuffy glances down at him, disdain in her fiery eyes. "Looks like it's up to Tuffy to save the day." She crouches down, raises her fists, then hollers—running at the trolls. The nearest troll roars back, then swats her away with his putrescent hand. Tuffy flies across the dining car and lands at Flagnad's feet.

"Oh, shit." I turn to the trolls, holding my suitcase in front of me like a shield.

Goat chirps as she soars over my head. "Looks like someone's growing up."

I glare at the eagle. "How is that helpful right now?"

The troll swats me and Anigo. We fly through the air, then land on top of Tuffy.

"You slime balls!" She wiggles underneath us. "Get off!"

As I struggle to detach myself from the pile of pathetic people, Flagnad floats over us and faces the trolls. He raises his hand and a beam of light shoots out of his palm. It hits the nearest troll, burning him to a crisp, then strikes the second. The trolls crumble into dust. The beam of light disappears. Flagnad wiggles his fingers, then blows on his smoking palm. He turns to us, still heaped on the floor, and smiles.

Goat lands beside the one booth that remains intact. She ruffles her feathers. "And the moral of the story is, Beauty is Only Skin Deep."

The back of my head throbs. I roll off the pathos pile and onto the cool, ash-streaked floor of the train. I sigh, massaging my neck. "Did anyone see where my suitcase went?"

Wind whips past my cheeks. I press my body against Flagnad's back, holding him tightly. Tuffy holds onto me— her soft hands clutch my elbows and her warm thighs press into my glutes. Goat's wings flap under my legs. I peer over her neck. Marshlands stretch out for miles below us. I wrench myself back and yell into Flagnad's ear. "All of this is Coalshaft?"

He turns his chin, yelling back. "Yes!"

"Even that tundra?"

"From sea to mountain, forest to sand, Coalshaft covers this whole land!"

I pause. The wind rips tears from my eyes, flinging them over my shoulder into Tuffy's golden hair. "Did you make that up?"

"No! She did!"

"She?"

"The Queen!"

"Of Coalshaft?"

"Yes! The Beast Mother, Birther of Dragons, Tyrannical Claw of the Southern Provinces, Exhumer of-"

"I get it!" A gnat flies into my mouth. I spit. My saliva flies into Tuffy's hair. "So, we have to kill the Queen to be reborn?"

"Yes! Only after she is dethroned will Coalshaft be free and its people truly alive!"

"Grand! So, how do we dethrone her?"

"A series of challenges!" Flagnad points over Goat's head. "The First approaches! Goat? Take us down!"

Goat tilts to the side and I squeeze my legs to stay on her slippery feathered back. We swoop lower and a manicured arena with flagpoles rising from its corners appears before us. I lift my head. "Flagnad?"

"Yes!"

"How are we all able to fit on Goat without falling off?"

"The First approaches! We're here!"

Goat backwings, then lands beside the manicured arena with a *thud!* Goat shakes her wings and we tumble to the earth. I climb to my feet as Tuffy and Anigo brush dirt off their khaki-green jackets. Goat throws my suitcase at me— she carried it in her talons during the flight.

I catch the bag then straighten, looking around. "Where's Bella?"

"Change your clothes, Duke." Flagnad floats towards the arena, beckoning us to join him. "This is a team challenge and uniforms are an essential part of game play."

"Have you seen Bella?"

"Change, Duke." Goat clucks, then nods at my suitcase. "Conform. You aren't special."

"But Bella-"

"Duke! Don't think about it too hard. Hurry!" Flagnad points towards the far side of the arena.

Four ethereal creatures stand in a line, watching us. Their robes of sapphire-shaded suede sway around their spindly ankles as their long white hair flows like waterfalls down their backs—Nordic Elves. The elves hold thick staffs in their delicate hands: canes, or some kind of stick. I squint, trying to make out the weapons, but the elves are too far away.

Flagnad corrals Tuffy and Anigo into a line on our side of the arena, then calls to me, "Get in your uniform. The First is about to begin!"

Hurrying, I unclasp my suitcase and pull out a shimmering opal jumpsuit. Shedding my jean jacket and board shorts I slip into the opal one-piece and shove my arms into the attached khaki-green jacket. I run to join our line, facing off with the opposing team. A vacuum cleaner lies on the grass at my feet.

Not a staff. Or a cane, or a stick.

Our battle weapons are vacuum cleaners.

I blink. "Am I supposed to do something with this?"

"Climb on!" Flagnad picks up his vacuum and mounts the hoover. Tuffy and Anigo follow. They rise into the sky to hover a foot above the ground. I turn—panicking—and watch the opposing elves do the same. My vacuum growls and nudges my toe with its intake port. Its rotating brush sucks on my sneaker. I step back. "Flagnad-"

"We ride!" Flagnad's vacuum jolts forward, followed by Tuffy and Anigo. The elves surge towards us, their vacuums growling.

I climb onto my cleaner. It purrs as my butt settles on its electric motor and I wrap my arms around its bag. "I don't know the rul-"

My team whizzes around the arena. I zoom behind, my vacuum happily growling as it sucks up grass, twigs and bits of leaves from two feet in the air. Flagnad approaches the northeast corner's flagpole, darts around a defending elf, then hoovers up the flag that waves from the top of the mast. Tuffy and Anigo cheer. The defending elf shrieks as their vacuum sputters and dies. The elf tumbles to the ground, kicks their broken vacuum, then lumbers away, disappearing into the rocky landscape that surrounds the manicured playing arena.

Goat flies over my head. "Watch out for flurries. Those are nimbostratus clouds accumulating."

I look up. The sun shines, the clouds drift lazily by, the sky is a clear blue.

"Duke!" Flagnad points behind me. "Take the southwest!"

Tuffy and Anigo approach the remaining three elves, ready for battle. My vacuum growls and surges towards the closest flagpole. We fly to the southern corner and suck the banner up. My vacuum purrs.

"Not too shabby, Duke!" Tuffy waves.

Anigo laughs, then points at the second elf as they storm off the arena, dragging their broken vacuum behind them. Then Anigo's eyes grow huge and his face warps with fright. "Behind you, Duke!"

Something slams into my body and I fall off my vacuum. It growls as I hit the ground. My vision goes dark.

A cool hand strokes my cheek. "Poor Duke. You missed the best part."

I open my eyes. Anigo's tiny face stares into mine, smiling tenderly. He strokes my cheek again, then looks over his shoulder. "Duke's awake. Duke's okay."

As I sit up I groan, expecting the worst; broken bones, torn ligaments, sprained—I stop. I roll my shoulder. I move my head from side to side. I feel great. No pain, no mangled body. "What happened?"

Angio pulls me to my feet. "We won." His dark brown eyes glint mischievously. "You looked good on that thing."

"Oh." I gulp, then stare at the ground. "Thanks."

Flagnad claps me on the back. "Ready for the Second challenge?"

Tuffy flips her hair. "Bring it on—it doesn't look scary to me." She points at a perfectly squared concrete building that's appeared on the edge of the arena. Its tall iron doors slowly open and Flagnad gestures for us to enter.

I look at Anigo, alarmed. "What's in there?"

He shrugs, then takes my hand. His fingers throb with heat. "I guess we'll have to face it together."

Flagnad repeats his magnanimous welcoming gesture. "The four of you must solve the Second and defeat the foe."

"The Queen?" My arms yank in their sockets as Anigo and Tuffy pull me towards the iron doors. Goat flies over our heads. I call back to Flagnad, who's smiling as the doors close behind us. "Is it the Queen, Flagnad?"

His voice makes it through the entranceway right before the doors slam. "It's a puzzle."

Silence.

I blink, trying to see through the darkness, but the square building prevents any light from penetrating its concrete boundaries.

Anigo's burning hand clutches mine. "What do you think the puzzle will be?"

Goat chirps. "They're always watching."

Tuffy laughs. Her voice echoes in the concrete space. "No one's watching us, seed brain. You can't see any-"

Searchlights snap on. I gasp, then squeeze my eyes shut to protect against the sudden glare.

"Duke! Look!"

I open my eyes. Anigo is staring at the ground—or what should be the ground and is, instead, twelve inches of garbage.

Trash.

"Gross." I lift my knee. My opal pant leg is soaked in sludge from the calf down. I shake my foot. A soggy piece of plastic wrap flies off my toe and sticks to the nearest wall. "What kind of puzzle is this?"

"Maybe it has something to do with those?" Anigo points at three cube-shaped bins lined up against the wall: one carbon black, one malachite green, one YInMn blue.

I trudge through the trash and look inside the blue bin. It's half full of cardboard, paper and tin cans. A glance inside the green bin reveals rotting fruits and vegetables, and the black contains a stinking assortment of garbage. I look over my shoulder at Anigo and Tuffy, then snort. "This isn't a puzzle. We have to sort this crap."

"We only have one planet." Goat lands on the green bin, clinging to the edge with her talons. "We're alone in the universe."

"We'd better get started." Tuffy picks up a milk carton and throws it into the blue. "No one else is going to do our dirty work."

"We can tackle the garbage together." Anigo wades through the calf-high muck, smiling at me. He pulls a bag of smelly refuse out of the sludge, then flings it into the black bin.

I sigh as I lean against the blue. "Some adventure. Chores?"

With a shrieking groan the walls of the building shudder, then start to move inwards—they push the sludge and trash into ever-mounting piles of death, closer and closer together, threatening to crush us.

"Now, this is a challenge!" Tuffy giggles as she rifles through the recycling, throwing cardboard cartons, plastic juice bottles and microwave dinner boxes into the blue.

Anigo pulls his tiny body up to the top of the growing garbage pile. "Organize from up here, Duke—then the pile won't swallow you." He grabs my hand and yanks me up.

I hang onto his arm as the walls close in. Tuffy laughs, then scrambles to the top of another expanding trash heap, separating the organics as she climbs.

Goat flies over our heads. "The aliens did this."

Tuffy tosses a banana peel into the green. "Goat! Help us."

Goat soars past. "We'll never make it."

Anigo throws a second bag of garbage into the black, then cups his mouth with his hand. "Goat! If you helped, we'd get out of here in no time."

Goat swoops by. "Viva la revolution."

I pick up a tin can and hurl it at the eagle. It bounces off her beak. She peers down at me through her piercing eye. The walls move closer. I point at the bins, which seem to float above the sludge as the room grows smaller. "Sort the trash, Goat!"

She cocks her head, scanning the room.

"Goat!" Anigo hollers. "The trash, the trash!"

The walls press in. Tuffy cackles, then whirls a ream of mulberry cabbage over her head like a lasso. "I've never felt so alive!"

Garbage fills my mouth. Compost covers my eyes. I feel the wind from Goat's wings move my fringe of hair. I yell again, one last time. "Help us, Goat! Sort the trash!"

The walls of the room press tight against my chest and I squeeze Anigo's burning hand. I think about all the things I'd never done, all the words I'd never said and all the chances I'd never chanced as the walls press tighter and tighter and-

The walls stop. With a shrieking groan they shudder, then retract. The room returns to its square shape—the trash neatly sorts into the three bins. A chute opens in the floor and sucks us in, sending us down a sliding tube that spits us out into an underground cavern.

Goat flies down the tube. She lands on a rock beside my foot. "Utopia is waiting."

I jump up—I have no injuries and am just a little bit stinky. "That was insane."

Tuffy laughs and throws herself into my arms. Anigo hoots, his voice bouncing off the walls of the cavern—then he kisses me.

On the mouth.

Holding Tuffy in one arm I lean into Anigo's kiss. His face is soft. He winds his fingers through my hair. Tuffy laughs breathlessly and presses her body into my side. I pull her closer as Anigo opens his lips. My cheeks boil. My stomach flips. My heart pounds and-

Goat clucks. "Triangles are so overdone."

I pull away, my cheeks flushing. Tuffy steps back. Anigo coughs and rubs side of his face. I turn, then stare around the cave. "So." I swallow. "Another challenge?"

"Yeah, another challenge." Anigo coughs, louder this time. "The Third. What do we have to do?"

"Check this out, schlebs." Tuffy kneels on the ground. She rubs the back of her neck, then pokes a pile of mud with a stick. We hurry to her side. She looks at Goat. Her ochre eyes twinkle. "Goblin feces."

"Ew!" Anigo pinches his nose. "Poo?"

Goat flips her wings. "The sun will burn you if you get too close."

I sigh. "There isn't any sun in here, Goat."

Goat takes off, flying into the air and landing on a rocky plateau high above our heads. "Then came the earthquakes."

A tumult of sound fills the cave. As one, we spin towards the roaring. Thousands of goblins pour out of a connecting tunnel, brandishing bristled scrub brushes, bottles of dish soap and yellow rubber gloves. The goblins scream, then chant as they run towards us. "Wash your dish-es! Wash your dish-es! Wash your-"

"NO!" I raise my hands in front of my body—like a shield. A beam of pure white light bursts from my palms. The light hits the horde of goblins and they explode, consumed by flame. They crumble into ash and their maintenance materials of mass mayhem clatter to the ground. I lower my hands. The beam of light evaporates. My palms throb. So does my head. I turn to my friends. They're frozen, staring.

Anigo grins. "That was sexy."

*Clap! Clap! Clap!* "Well done, kiddies." Flagnad floats out of the tunnel, slowly striking his hands together. He smiles, then snaps his fingers.

I blink. It's night. We're sitting around a campfire at the base of a hideous Pine. The stars sparkle overhead. The flames crackle merrily, casting a warm glow on Tuffy, Anigo and Flagnad's faces. Goat perches on the lowest branch of the Pine, crunching on a bone. She coughs—chokes—and a rodent skull falls onto the grass under the tree. She scratches her beak with her talon, then chirps. "And the moral of the story is, Slow and Steady Wins the Race."

Flagnad smiles, delicate and sensuous. "Get some rest. Tomorrow's another big day."

I stare up at the castle doors that loom over my head. Runes crawl along the edges of the entrance, weighty with power. I nod grimly as I attempt to translate the inscription.

SEIROTS NAIPOTSYD ROF SELCIHEV
LUFREDNOW ERA
SKOOB NOITCIF ECNEICS DNA YSATNAF

I turn to Flagnad, who's tracing the words with his eyes. I swallow, then nudge him with my elbow. "Can we talk for a minute?"

Flagnad's smile wavers. He gestures to a boulder. I sit, worrying the hem of my jacket between my fingers. Flagnad frowns, then sits beside me. "What's on your mind?"

"What happened yesterday? In the goblin cave." I look at my hands. They're fine—I still feel better than ever—but the power residing within them frightens me. I want answers.

Flagnad nods. "I've been waiting for this day for a long time." He sighs, then pats my knee. "When you were young you were born into a tragic fate. Your mother, a beautiful princess, fell in love with a fiendishly vile man. She gave birth to his child—you—but you couldn't remain with her. The fiendishly vile man wanted you dead, so she had to send you away. She sent you to the world you know—Old York City." He pauses. Tears prick at the corners of his eyes.

I swallow the lump that's formed in my throat. "My birth mother is a princess?"

Flagnad shakes his head. "Was a princess. Your father killed her, not long after you were sent away."

"No!"

"I hate to be the one to tell you this, but it's true. You're here to right the wrongs that were done to your mother. Kill Queen Morda and return Coalshaft to its rightful state."

"And this power?" I clench my hands. "Is it hers? Or is it-" I look up. "His."

"Your power is yours, and yours alone. Only you can wield its true potential." Flagnad wipes his eyes. "I despise being the one to tell you this, but it's true."

I nod, accepting my destiny. "And the others?"

Flagnad turns. "What?"

"The others." I frown. "Tuffy and Anigo. Why are they here?"

Flagnad sighs, then pats my knee. "Tuffy is a Killer. She comes from an ancient line of female warriors, destined to fight an eternal battle between good and evil." He pauses. Tears run down his cheeks. "She must work with you to kill Queen Morda and return Coalshaft to its rightful state."

"That's awful." I stare at my hands. "What a terrible burden." I frown, then look up. "And Anigo?"

Flagnad sighs. He pats my knee. "Anigo is an exiled emperor from a faraway land. His twelve-fingered uncle usurped his throne and married his mother, then cursed his sister with the tail of a fish. Anigo's aunt hid him in a basket of reeds and sent him across the ocean with only a tiger for a companion. Anigo was forced to kill his companion to stay alive, then teach himself mastery of the sword so he could avenge his father's death. After he turns twenty-one and frees the genie from his ancestral lamp the Wheel will align with the present and the Timeclock will reset and Winter will come and the Loom will shuttle inevitably forward." He pauses. Snot streams out of his nose. "Anigo must work with you to kill Queen Morda and return Coalshaft to its rightful state."

My head pounds. Pain shoots up my jawline. I massage the side of my face, squinting at Flagnad. "Wait. Really?"

Goat dives out of the sky and lands beside me. "Don't think about it too hard."


The sound of dripping water echoes down the stony hallway. Wall torches flicker as I pass them by. I walk silently, stealthily approaching the castle's throne room. A scream rents the cold night air, ricocheting off the castle walls. Cruel mocking laughter follows and the sound of footsteps thump toward me. I stop, then press my back into the stone wall.

A gorgeous maiden with a thick braid and a silver pin attached to her lapel hurtles around the corner. She sees me, gasps, then runs to my side. She throws her bow and arrow to the stone floor and falls into my arms, sobbing. "Get me out of here! Please! She's horrible! I can't-"

"Shhh." I stroke her braid. "Don't be afraid. I'll protect you." I look down at her black coroneted head. She lifts her face, gazing into my eyes. Her olive complexion is blotchy with fear, her grey eyes clouded with terror. I rub her back. "Tell me your name and I'll help you."

"Hibiscus." She smiles, shakily. "My name is Hibiscus."

I touch the tip of her nose with my finger. "Boop." She giggles. I wipe a tear from her olive eyeball. "I'm here now, Hibiscus."

"Oh, thank you." She snuggles into my chest.

I smile, then step away. "Just head down the hall, take your first left, go down the stairs to the drawing room, turn right, go through the tapestry with Hosborn the Goblin King on it—Hosborn the Goblin King, not his brother, Nosborn, he was only a prince—then take another left, two more rights, one more left and you'll find them. My friends." I nod, graciously. "They'll help you."

Hibiscus blinks. "What?"

I point. "Just head down the hall, take your first left, go down the stairs to the drawing room, turn right-"

"No." Hibiscus holds up her hand, frowning. "Aren't you coming with me?"

I chuckle. "I have to kill Queen Morda."

"Oh." Hibiscus looks around, then back at me. "So... um, your friends are-"

"In the armoury." I nod. "I said that."

"Uh, no. I don't think you did, actuall-"

"I don't have time for this." I turn, stalking towards the cruel mocking laugher. "Just go down the hall."

"Thanks?" Hibiscus' voice follows me around a cobblestone corner. "I guess?"

Goat flies over my head. She clucks as we make our way around another cobblestone corner. "There's nothing like classical totalitarian architecture."

We turn the final cobblestone corner and stop in front of an archway. Carved into its keystone is an image of a grotesque Oak. Shaking my head to dispel the scrofulous shrub from my thoughts, I flex my fingers, then shake out my hands—I'm ready. I leap under the archway and into the throne room, palms extended. There she is. Queen Morda.

The evil Queen sits on her throne of bones, blood fountaining out of the eye sockets of her victims like-

"Are you Duke?"

I drop my arms. The Queen walks towards me, hands outstretched. I scuttle back, raising my palms again. "One more step and I'll blast you to smithereens, pardner!"

Goat swoops over my head to land on the throne of bones. "Wrong genre, pardner."

"Duke!" The Queen trots towards me—beautiful and radiant. She gathers me in a warm embrace. "My darling."

I writhe in her clutches. My head starts to pound. "Get off me!"

"My darling!" Queen Morda steps back. She looks confused. I feel confused. The Queen tucks her hair behind her ears. "Darling, don't you know who I am?"

My heart stops. Of course I know who she is. A part of me has known the whole time. "Mom."

"My baby!" My mother opens her arms and I fall into her hug, crying with my entire heart. My mother runs her long fingernails through my hair, then touches the tip of my nose. "Boop." I giggle. My mother flips her golden curls. "We need to catch up, my darling. Come. Sit with mommy."

I sit on my mother's knee. She coos in my ear, popping bonbons in my mouth. "Be a good baby and listen to my story."

"Yes, Mom-Mom."

"Such a sweet baby." She places a chocolate on my tongue. "Once upon a time I was a princess. But I fell in love with a fiendishly vile man who stole my throne and broke my heart. Then you were born." She places a sugar-snap in my mouth. "The fiendishly vile man was too terrible and I had to send you away so you could be safe. The prophecy said you would return to me, so I knew you would be alright." She places a sour jelly between my lips. "Then I was able to banish the fiendishly vile man by making a deal with the Dragon Overlord."

"Who is he, Mommy?"

"Hush, darling. Listen to mommy's story. So, I went to the Dragon Overlord and promised that if he banished the fiendishly vile man from my Queendom I would bear his children."

"Gross. Germs."

"Hush, darling. I'm getting to the good part." She places a liquorice whip between my teeth. "I gave birth to thousands of his dragon children. We grew a dragon family and raised a dragon army which turned into a dragon brigade that has kept the peace in Coalshaft these past seventeen years."

"Wow!"

"I know!"

"What about the fiendishly vile man?"

"Hush, darling." She places a gumball down my throat. "The fiendishly vile man was banished. And all is right with the world."

"Yay!" I clap my hands together.

"Yes, it's all very wonderful." My mother fondles my earlobe. "But I need your help. My dragon sentries told me that the fiendishly vile man has returned. He wants to kill me and steal my throne. You have to-"

"Ow!" I bend over, clutching the sides of my face.

The Queen leans closer. "What's wrong?"

"My head." The pain in my jaw stabs, right beside my ear. "It hurts."

"Kid? Hey—are you okay?"

"OW! Shit. No."

"Shit. Can I do something?"

"AH! Holy crap!" I grab my head. "Can you—AHHH! I don't know, can you call for help? Call the connect0-"

Flagnad bursts into the throne room.

Goat swoops down. "Death to the ruling class! Down with peasants! Kill the witches!"

Anigo runs to my side, waving a dueling foil over his head. "Get away from her! She's Queen Morda!"

"No, it's—ow!" I bat Anigo away, holding the sides of my face and climbing off the Queen's lap. "Something's wrong."

Anigo drops his foil. "What's wrong?"

"Something—ow!"

Anigo grabs my hand. "Are you okay?"

"I'm fine, but we have to get out of here." The pain shoots to the top of my head. "Zap! Where's Tuffy?"

"She disappeared in the armoury. Are you sure you're okay? You don't look so good."

Flagnad strides across the throne room and pushes the Queen to the floor. She screams, clawing at her face. "My dragon babies! What have you done to them?"

I turn, still bent over. Crowding into the throne room are hundreds of tiny dragons, about the size of puppies. They pant—slimy tongues loll out of their scaly mouths as they gaze at Flagnad with adoring eyes.

The wizard laughs, fiendish and vile. "You stupid woman. Children have no loyalty. They respect power, not a mother's womb."

"NO!" The Queen writhes on the ground, tearing at the bodice of her dress. Her breasts burst from their restrictive bindings. The air billowing in from the deserted hallway touch her nipples and they harden as the Queen scrambles to her knees. She gathers her skirts around her hips, then slides onto her back. The Queen's cold-pricked breasts point towards the throne of death as she reaches between her open legs, arches her spine, then rocks her pelvis against the icy tiled floor. A moan curls out of her mouth. My stomach clenches, then turns cold.

Angio whispers in my ear. "Mothers. Am I right?"

"AHHH!" I grab my head.

Anigo crouches beside me. "I've been getting headaches, too. Maybe they're a side effect?"

"ANIGO!" My brain is about to burst. Raising my palms in front of me I straighten, gritting my teeth against the pain. I turn to Anigo, desperate for a shoulder to lean on.

He's gone.

"ZAP!" I turn to face the dragon troops, who've fallen on the Queen's writhing body and are tearing it to shreds.

Goat clucks. "And the moral of the story is, You Cannot Escape Your Fa-"

Goat disappears, mid-downstroke.

Flagnad raises his hands to the sky as the dragon battalion cavort around the throne room, strips of the Queen's dress lolling out of their mouths. Flagnad laughs and laughs and laughs. I have to stop this. I brace myself for the fire.


A beam of pure white light shoots out my palms. The throne room fills with blinding iridescent rays, casting a frosty glare on the dragons and their fiendishly vile master before they dissolve into nothingness. The light dims.

The room is empty.

I lie on the frozen floor of the throne room, holding my head and sobbing. "It wasn't supposed to be like this. What is happening? Can anyone hear me? I paid good money for this game, it's not supposed to hurt. My head! Oh god, my head. Someone get me out of here! HELP M-"

Mr. Lee removed the connect0-chip from his temple. "Mr. Ice? We lost another campaign."

Mr. Ice turned around. "Which game?"

"Dragon Mountain, sir."

Mr. Ice frowned. "How many losses this quarter? In total."

"Eighty-four thousand, sir."

"Same problem as the others?"

"Yes, sir. Insects chew through the connect0-casings and eat our clients while they're still alive."

"Connect0-clients, Mr. Lee."

"My apologies, sir."

"How?"

"Pardon me, sir?"

"How did the insects eat these particular connect0-clients?"

"Burrowed into the connect0-clients' brains through their ear canals, sir. Same as the other campaigns. I mean, connect0-campaigns."

"Darn." Mr. Ice squeezed his eyes shut. "What has the connect0-carpenter team decided to do about it?"

"A rebuild, sir. We'll go dark across the globe next week so the connect0-contractors can replace the connect0-casings."

"What's the new material?"

"A hybrid of plastic and silicon, sir."

"What's that going to cost?"

"Forty-three trillion."

"Phooey." Mr. Ice opened his eyes. "Can we include some kind of connect0-cranial protection in the upgrade? Stop the insects from making it to the connect0-clients' heads?"

"That'll be an additional six trillion, sir."

"Hmmm." Mr. Ice ran his fingers through his hair. "Can we sell more ad space?"

"We've been getting complaints about the advertisements, sir. Apparently, they distract the gamers."

Mr. Ice scowled. "Connect0-clients, Mr. Lee. Not gamers."

"Yes, sir." Mr. Lee's eyes unfocused as he contacted the accounting department through his Neurachain. "Ms. Patel says it will cost us less to do the upgrades than to keep losing clients. I mean, connect0-clients. Sir."

Mr. Ice sighed. "Cut the headgear and go forward with the hybrid connect0-casings." His eyes locked on Lee's. "Will they know? When the rebuild is happening?"

"No, sir. When the games go dark everyone loses connect0-consciousness. It'll return after we reboot."

"Good." Mr. Ice turned to the connect0-cinema that projected the gaming world to the connect0-coders that filled the connect0-cyber room. He watched his connect0-clients enjoying their meta moments and felt his heart lift. "I'd like to take some time to honour the lives of those whom we have recently lost. The destruction of a connect0-campaign is a significant hit to our connect0-community.

Mr. Lee? Can you arrange the appropriate accommodations?"

"Yes, sir."

"Thank you." Mr. Ice looked over his shoulder. "And tell the connect0-carpenters and connect0-contractors that the next series of connect0-casings had better be a significant improvement over the last. Get them to check the outside of the connect0-crypts as well. We can't afford to lose another life. The cost is too high."

Mr. Ice placed his connect0-chip on his temple, brushed a lock of silver hair off his brow, then merged with the gaming world. The Old York City sidewalk flickered. Mr. Ice scratched his temple, adjusting the connect0-chip. The flickering stopped. He nodded to the connect0-characters passing him on the street as they made their way to the next real-life adventure fantasy.

Mr. Ice strode down the city sidewalk, pushed open the door to his Video Game Emporium, and smiled. "Life is our most precious commodity."

# YOU KNOW WHAT I THINK?

# 13

"Raylyn? Sweetheart, we need to talk."

Raylyn looked up from his plate. A piece of broccoli hung limply from his fork. He dropped the utensil and it clattered against the side of his porcelain dish. "What did I do?"

"Nothing, sweetheart, you didn't do anything." His mum pulled her dining chair closer. She leaned over the table, then patted his hand. "We love you so much."

"That's not true." His father scowled from his seat at the head of the table. "Oh. No, we love you, but you did do something. Something wrong. Again."

Raylyn slumped. His shoulders curved downwards as his chin lifted up towards his mum's face. "What?"

His mum stroked his wrist. "Your teacher called."

His sister giggled. "You are such a clod."

His father scowled. "Don't be rude."

Raylyn felt a bit better.

"Sweetheart." His mum squeezed his fingers. "Mr. Garcia called because you broke the law."

"We have to discuss this as a family now. Ryland-"

"Raylyn, Frank."

"That's what I said. Ryland, this behaviour has happened too many times. You've gone too far."

Raylyn frowned, trying to remember what he'd done wrong that day. "It was my turn to feed Doctor Hamster, I promise. And he likes when I give him extra treats. It's not my fault he got so sick."

"No, sweetheart." His mum slid her hands into her lap. "This isn't about Doctor Hamster."

"Though we are going to discuss your class rodent's health after this conversation."

"Mr. Garcia called because you shared your opinion. Out loud. For the third time."

"Oh, yeah." Raylyn blushed. "Sorry."

"What happened?" His sister grinned. A broccoli floret dangled off the side of her lip. "What'd he do, Mummy?"

"It doesn't matter what happened, what matters is it can't happen again." His mum leaned over the table. "You understand that. Don't you? Ray-Ray?"

"Must you call the boy that insufferable name?"

"I understand." Raylyn picked up his fork, then stuffed his broccoli into his mouth. "I wonf du ib ahgin."

"Sorry, sweetheart?"

"Chew before you speak. You aren't an animal."

Raylyn swallowed. "I won't do it again."

His mum smiled. "There. I knew you'd understand." She turned to nod at his father. "See? No big conversation needed. Ray-Ray won't share his opinions anymore."

"I don't believe it." His father scowled. "It's time to have… The Talk."

His mum hissed. She grabbed Raylyn's fingers, crushing them in her grasp. "Not The Talk. It's too soon. They're both still so young. Can't we wait a few more years?"

"A stampede of ostriches paraded through the middle school this afternoon and it was your son's fault. We don't have a few more years, Clare."

"Alright." His mum released his throbbing fingers, then clenched her hands in her lap. "But can't the children finish their dinner first?"

"No." His father leaned back in his chair, surveying the dining room through his bespectacled eyes. "Now, Clare. Start."

His mum sighed. "Alright. Ray-Ray? Harpy-bean? We want you to know how much we love you-"

"You said that already."

"-and it's important to us that this is an open, honest conversation. We know some of the things in The Talk will feel uncomfortable-"

"They've seen worse on YouTube, Clare. Please get to the point."

"-but this is a safe environment and we want you to trust us. After we have The Talk, you are allowed to ask us anything you want."

His sister grinned. "Anything?"

"Anything within reason." His father nodded. "Anything appropriate."

"Yes, Harpy-bean." His mum nodded. "Anything. You understand? Ray-Ray?"

Raylyn stared at the dinner growing cold on his plate. He sighed. "Yeah."

"Good." His father nodded. "Clare?"

"Alright." His mum's hands trembled. "Well, first we want you to know how your father and I feel about sharing opinions. I was raised in a house that never stated specific thoughts or feelings out loud. It was too dangerous."

"My father allowed me and my brothers to share our opinions with people we trusted. But only opinions where the consequences would be small."

"Really?" His sister wiggled on her seat. "We can share some of our opinions?"

"Frank, I don't think they can handle that kind of discretion at their age. Don't you think we should keep it simple? That worked best with my sisters and-"

"You see, Harpo-"

"Harper, hon."

"That's what I said. You see, Harpo, I believe that you are smart, no matter how old you are. I believe you can tell the difference between a small opinion with little consequence and a large opinion with damaging consequences. Like Ryland's, this afternoon."

"I didn't know the ostriches would run through the school, Dad."

"See, Frank? Choice is too hard, too much trouble, they're too young and-"

"No, Clare. The trouble is that Ryland isn't sensible. If you took the time, son, to pause before you said your opinions out loud you might know what to say, when to say it, who to say it to, why it's important to say what you say when you think you should say it and-"

"Frank!"

"What kinds of opinions did you say out loud, Daddy?"

"Great question, Harpo." His father smiled. "See, Clare? Most children can handle discretion. Ryland just has to learn." His father turned to his sister, gesturing as he lectured. "There are many acceptable opinions to share. Like that you prefer a different type of toothpaste. Or you'd rather your shoelaces be a different colour."

"So…" Harper picked her lip. "I could say that I think-"

His mum threw her body over the table, clapping her hand over Harper's mouth. "Frank! Do you have any idea what could have just happened?"

Raylyn smirked as he watched Harper squirm in his mum's grip, vocalizing unintelligibly, muted by his mum's reedy fingers.

Harper jerked her head and his mum paled. She removed her hand and pulled herself back over the table. "Sorry, Harpy-bean. I was just scared."

Harper rubbed her mouth. "Maybe I'm not ready to share my opinion."

"Not so fast." His father leaned backwards over his seat, towards the buffet. Opening a drawer with one hand he removed a small pad and pen, then pushed the paper set across the table to Harper. "Write down what you were going to say. Then we can decide if it's acceptable to share out loud."

"Frank!"

"Give her the chance, Clare." His father tapped the side of his glasses. "We are here to oversee."

"Alright." His mum stood. She grabbed their dinner plates and clipped towards the kitchen on her cream-coloured heels.

Raylyn watched sadly as his food was removed and his sister scribbled on the pad. Harper's grin grew with impish glee as she wrote, eyes intent on the page. His mum finished clearing, then stood behind her chair—fingers gripping the back of the seat and her toe tapping anxiously.

"Done!" Harper pushed the pad across the table.

His father lifted the page, adjusted his spectacles, then smiled. "This seems perfectly reasonable. Say it."

"Frank!"

"Say it, Harpo." A low growl filled the room, coming from his father's chest. "Say it."

His mum turned white. Harper smirked, then cleared her throat. "I think Raylyn would look better with purple hair."

His mum shrieked.

Raising a hand to his head, Raylyn pulled down the longest side of his bangs and squinted. Sure enough, his hair had changed from its sandy brown colour to a deep indigo. He sighed. "So, it's not okay for me to think that the school should have ostriches as mascots, but it is okay for me to look cringey?"

Harper hooted, clapping her hands together. "You look so good! What else can I say, Daddy?"

"No!" His mum wiped her nose with the back of her hand. "Turn him back, Harpy-bean, please. And stop this. No good comes from sharing your opinion."

"For once, I agree with your mother, Harpo." His father smiled. "Change it back."

"Fine." Harper rolled her eyes, then glared at the ceiling. "I think Raylyn should have boring old brown hair."

Raylyn pulled down on his bangs. His hair was back to brown. Not the exact same shade as before—it was a little less shiny, a little less rich, a little more muted, but at least it wasn't ugly, fluorescent, concord-grape purple. "Thanks?"

"Now that you've made your point, Frank, can we please agree that the children should never share their opinions? Ever? It worked for my family—and for countless other people. It's more than fine for our family, too."

"This is a democratic household, Clare. We vote. Who thinks you should be allowed to share small, safe opinions?"

Harper thrust her hand into the air. Raylyn shrugged, then did the same.

His mum wiped her eyes. "This won't end well."

"Now that we've agreed, let's move on. Clare? Please tell the children about the dangers of listening to other people."

His mum took a deep shuddering breath, then clipped into the kitchen. Raylyn could hear her blowing her nose, loudly. Then she clipped back into the dining room, red-eyed, pink-nosed and puffy-cheeked. She looked like Aunt Ruth on Boxing Day.

His mum sank onto her chair and took another breath. "Alright. If you're going to be sharing opinions—small ones!—it's important to know what your opinions are. So don't listen to anyone else. Ever! People will confuse you and you'll say things you don't mean."

"Like when Uncle Ashmar said he thought Auntie Ruth should die because Cousin Willis said she ate the last of the cranberry tarts?"

"Exactly, Harpy-bean." His mum shivered. "That was a horrible Christmas."

"Or when Mrs. Skerdpunts said she thought Shelly was crazy and the school counsellor had to lock Shelly in the calming closet until her daddies picked her up?"

"Right. It's not just family you need to be wary of." His father ticked off the list on his fingers. "Beware what your gymnastic teacher tells you, Harpo, what your violin instructor tell you, Ryland, what your hockey coaches say, and that weirdo sitter we have to use when Aunt Bea goes out of town-"

"What those TokTik influenzas show you on their rods-"

"-what the CBTV newscasters report, those rubes are morons-"

"-what Nana says when she's had too many edibles-"

"-what that idiotic singer with the big boobs and giant nose sings about, she doesn't have half a brain in her head-"

"-and be careful about Lila Gahcip's mother, I know she seems fun on field trips but Sinclair Toksic said she secretly feeds coyotes in the wintertime-"

"-and never—never!—trust the information that your friends and classmates tell you." His father scowled. "Really, you should just listen to us. Any thought coming from someone younger than forty-five is nonsensical. And if they don't have a college degree, they might as well be coke addicts and hipsters."

"What's coke?"

"It's one of those sugary sodas the Jointly quadruplets drink."

"No, Clare. I meant the hard drug."

"Don't tell them what cocaine is, Frank!"

"Cocaine isn't a thing anymore, Mum."

"And how would you know that, Ray-Ray? Who have you been talking to?"

"No one, but-"

"Enough!" His father slammed his hand on the table. "Enough. Clare? Outline the Four Cs."

His mum's hands quivered. "Alright. The Four Cs are the rules you need to follow if you're going to say your opinions out loud. They stand for Correct, Certain, Clear and Control. You have to say Correct words-"

"So, this afternoon when you said you wanted your school to have ostrich mascots, what you meant was that you wanted your school to have one ostrich mascot safely tethered in the playground and kept away from humans. Right, Ryland?"

"Sure."

His mum nodded. "Certain means you are aware of all the things that will happen when you share your opinion."

"So, you needed to know that a pack of wild ostriches would rampage through your school hallway, destroy your coat cubbies, overturn the new lunch tables that cost the school board zillions of taxpayer dollars, start mating in the gym-"

"There's no way I could have known they would do all that!"

"Then you shouldn't have shared that opinion." His mum's teary eyes glinted in the dining room chandelier's light. "Right, sweetheart?"

"Sure."

"Tell them about Clear, Clare."

"That's funny." Raising her tiny fist Harper banged out a steady beat on the table. "Clear Clare. Clear Clare. Clear Clare. Clear-"

"Stop it!" Raylyn jumped to his feet, overturning his chair as he glared at his sister. "I think you are bitch!"

"NO!" His mum screamed as a loud *pop!* resounded in the room and Harper disappeared. On her chair sat a large, rotund Rottweiler, teats engorged, drool dribbling out the corner of her square-jawed mouth and onto the floor.

"Ray-Ray." His mum whimpered. "How could you say that? She's about to give birth."

With a whine, the dog leapt to the ground and crouched under the table, groaning and panting with labour pains.

His father thundered, striking palm upraised. "Young man, you turn her back! Right now!"

"Be Clear, sweetheart." His mum stared at the birthing beast, eyes wide with panic. "Be specific. One wrong word and Harpy-bean will be gone forever."

Raylyn sighed. He pulled on a piece of his boring old brown hair. "I think Harper is my sister. A normal, nine-year-old girl with normal black hair, who was born on May 14, 2036."

*Pop!*

Harper crawled out from under the table. "That was weird. Also, we have a puppy." She held a fluid-soaked baby Rotweiller in her outstretched hands. Giggling, she stroked the crown of its head with her forefinger. "I'm going to name him Ryland."

"Go get Ryland cleaned up, Harpy-bean." His mum sank onto her chair. She buried her face in her hands. "Towels are in the bathroom closet."

As Harper skipped from the room with the mewling pup Raylyn's father scowled. "Sit."

Raylyn sat, shoulders slumped.

"Look at me."

Raylyn looked up, lifting his chin towards his father.

"Listen." His father took a breath while his mum quietly whimpered. "The last lesson you need to learn is how to say 'no'. That's Control."

His mum looked up. She wiped her eyes and smiled, blinking through her tears. "Yes, Ray-Ray. That lesson is so important. Show him the dance, Frank."

His father pushed himself to his feet. "Stand up, Ryland. Copy what I do."

Raylyn stood, warily watching his father, who started performing a strange series of movements while chanting a rhyme in a singsong voice. Raylyn's stomach clenched. The Talk was bizarre, but this was worse: his stoic, logical dad never indulged in the soft arts. Raylyn wished he could run from the room and heave his mediocre dinner in the toilet—which would be better than mimicking his cold-fish parent—but, instead, he swallowed and did his best to keep up.

His father flailed and sung, limp-limbed and feeble-voiced.

*"When you're asked to share a thought* [finger to temple]

*"And you're not sure what to say* [shake head once]

*"Like where you want to eat* [fist in mouth]

*"Or how you'd like to pray* [hands in peak]

*"Here's a courteous response* [fingers in the air]

*"To keep the nosey-noos at bay:* [hips side to side]

*"No. "*

His father stopped.

Raylyn waited.

His father raised his eyebrows, staring at him expectantly.

Raylyn dropped his hands. "No?"

"No." His father nodded, then sat down. "Just no."

"Just no?"

"Yes."

"If someone asks to hear my opinion, I just tell them no?"

"Yes."

Raylyn frowned. "Isn't that rude?"

"Oh, no, sweetheart." His mum's smile wavered. "It's the kindest thing. Some people have no boundaries and they don't always know what will happen when they ask you to say what you think."

"But what if they need to know my opinion? To make a decision or something. What if my opinion is important?"

His father sighed. "Opinions are never important. They just make life interesting, if used sparingly. There's no need to make this complicated, Ryland. Just say no. Oh, and don't ask to hear anyone else's opinion. Appalling nonsense. You can think for yourself without needing to consult a zillion sources. People require validation for the most ridiculous things these days-"

"But-" Raylyn sat, tucking his legs under his chair. "But what if saying my opinion helps me? So I can go to the university I want. Or get the degree I want. Or marry who I want. Aren't my opinions about those things important? Shouldn't I-"

"You don't have to worry about that, sweetheart."

"Those decisions will be made for you. By us. When you're older."

"So-" Raylyn frowned at the tabletop. "So, you don't care what I think about that stuff? About how I want my life to be after I move out?"

"Of course we care!" His mum cried into her hands. "I knew it was too soon to have The Talk."

His father frowned. "What does us caring about you have to do with you sharing your opinions, Ryland?"

"Won't I need to say what I think when I live by myself?" Raylyn's stomach flipped. "Or when I'm with my friends? When I grow up?"

"You'll know how to manage those details later." His father glared. "Stop overpreparing for a future you know nothing about."

"But-" Raylyn's stomach grumbled. "So, when I'm older, I'll just... know. What to say, when to say it, who to say it to, and why it's important to say what you say when you think you should say it?"

"Fantastic, Ryland. You're showing a firm grasp of the concept. You can start sharing small opinions, now."

"Sure. But with big opinions, or if someone asks for my opinion, I say-"

"No."

"Yes, sweetheart, no. It's much safer."

"No." Raylyn nodded. His stomach churned. "Just no."

"Fantastic."

"Good job, sweetheart. See, Frank? I knew he'd understand."

"But The Talk helped him understand. See, Clare?"

"Of course, Frank. And my name is Frances. Frances, Frank. Frances." His mum pulled her chair closer, leaning over the table and patting his hand. "Do you have any thoughts, Ray-Ray? About The Talk?"

"No."

His father guffawed. "That's what I like to hear." He adjusted his frames, which had slipped down the bridge of his nose. "Fantastic, son. I can confidently tell Mr. Garcia you learned your lesson. No more trouble at school."

Raylyn nodded.

His mum smiled, then clipped into the kitchen. She grabbed a rag from the sink, returned to the living room, then crawled under the table and began wiping up the canine birthing fluid that was starting to fill the room with a pungent, sourish smell. His father leaned back in his chair, surveying Raylyn through his bespectacled eyes. He grinned, pushed his chair away from the table, then adjusted his frames as he strode from the room.

Raylyn stood. "You know what I think?"

His parents froze. One of his father's legs hung in the air. One of his mum's hands clutched the soggy rag.

Raylyn took a breath. "I think-"

Stefanie Barnfather is an independent writer in Canada. Previously, she taught high school arts and inclusive education, and volunteered her artistry to support local theatre and production companies. Ms. Barnfather graduated with honours from Sheridan Institute's Music Theatre - Performance program and has a BFA and BED in secondary fine arts from the University of Calgary. When she isn't writing, she enjoys painting, hiking and spending time with her husband and pug.

Much thanks to Bruce Lyall, Alex Lyall and Judy Gilbert for lending this book their editing talents. Thank you to Marisa Roggeveen for modelling for the book cover, and to Matthew Barnfather for being an objective and critical voice throughout the publishing process.

You can follow @stefbarnfather on Instagram, Twitter, Pinterest, LinkedIn and YouTube or visit Ms. Barnfather's website: www.stefaniebarnfather.com

Manufactured by Amazon.ca
Bolton, ON